Live from New York, It's LENA SHARPE

Courtney
Litz

Live from New York, It's LENA SHARPE

RED
DRESS
INK
TM

First edition October 2004

LIVE FROM NEW YORK, IT'S LENA SHARPE

A Red Dress Ink novel

ISBN 0-373-25073-8

www.RedDressInk.com

Printed in U.S.A.

For Mom, Dad and Paige

Special thanks to:

My parents, Edward and Mary Litz,
and my sister, Paige Litz.

And:
Josh Horowitz, Alexandra Bresnan,
Charlotte Morgan, Renee Kaplan, Jennifer Cohan
and Sarah Jones.

Also:
My sincere thanks to Isabel Swift, Margaret Marbury
and Farrin Jacobs for their encouragement
and invaluable editorial guidance.

chapter 1

Do you ever have those moments when you wonder how the many twists and turns in your life have brought you to a particular (usually disappointing) juncture? This was one of those moments.

5,4,3,2,1...Rolling

Cue Music—

Kelly Karaway, Host: Hello and welcome to *Face to Face.* I'm your host, Kelly Karaway. Each week for our special segment, "Reinventions," we spotlight a different celebrity as you've *never* seen them before. Last week, we saddled up our horse and joined your favorite heartthrob and mine, Harrison Ford, as he gave us a private peek at his other starring role—as a Montana cattle rancher. Boy, that was worth suffering a few saddle sores for, wasn't it, ladies! And this week, we've got a special treat for all you *guys* out there! You know her as the breakout WB star and four-time *Maxim* cover girl, but tonight on "Reinventions," we'll show you how actress Sienna Skye has *reinvented* her spirituality. Hello and welcome, Ms. Sienna Skye!

Sienna Skye: Thanks, Kelly. It's so great to be here.

Kelly Karaway: This past year has been a crazy one for you, hasn't it? Tell us, if you can, what is it like to be Sienna Skye?

Sienna Skye: Well, it's very, very difficult. I'll be honest with you, Kelly, when I'm working, I'm just giving and giving, and sometimes I just feel like I don't have anything left, you know? Like when I was playing Cassidy—

Kelly Karaway: Excuse me, Sienna, I just need to explain to the audience in case they've been in a coma for the last six months—Cassidy was your character in the WB movie of the week, *Cassidy's Crisis* and she was both a stripper *and* a single mom.

Sienna Skye: That's right. And you know, Kelly, sometimes I would come home from the set and I would be so immersed in the character that I would just feel like I *was* a stripper, you know…

Kelly Karaway: Mmm, that's fascinating, Sienna.

Sienna Skye: And so when Rafe asked me to chant with him…

Kelly Karaway: And Rafe would be…

Sienna Skye: He's my colorist, but he's also just so much more to me, Kelly. Anyway, Rafe introduced me to Buddhism and that has made all the difference.

Kelly Karaway: That's just *fascinating* Sienna, really. So what is it about Buddhism that works for you? Can you explain it?

Sienna Skye: I feel like, well, I feel like I can *breathe* again. Buddha, he's just my number one guy right now.

Kelly Karaway: Oh, that's so beautiful I can't even stand it. Thank you so much for sharing that with us, Sienna, really.

And today, we've got a special treat for all our viewers be-
cause Sienna's going to show us her extensive and exquisite
collection of Buddha figures!
Sienna Skye: That's right.
[Wide shot as camera pans across Buddha display.]
Kelly Karaway: Now, I absolutely adore this one. Look at
those shiny eyes!
[Close-up on Buddha.]
Sienna Skye: Well, that's a very sentimental one, actually.
The eyes are made from sequins taken from my stripper cos-
tume in *Cassidy's Crisis.*
Kelly Karaway: That is *fascinating,* Sienna. Sal, could you just
move in for a close-up on this one, please… Oh, for Christ
sake, Cut! Who put this glass of water here? Lena! Who the
hell's in charge here?
CUT

"Lena! Lena! Stop daydreaming!"

I was deep into a conversation with Martin Scorsese and
Joan Didion, so I didn't hear Sal yelling at me. Marty was
after me to see his newest film and Joan just couldn't stop
raving about my latest think piece for the *Sunday Times.* Such
a sweetheart, that Joan.

"Hey, Lena, you gotta clean this crap up. I don't got all
day here," Sal, and I don't mean Salman Rushdie, barked at
me between bites of his pastrami sandwich.

And that's when I started wondering: How did I get here?
To this moment? How had all the events in my life added
up to this? In theory, I was a television producer working
on a location shoot in downtown Manhattan. In reality, I
had been rearranging a TV starlet's glittering Buddhas for
the past four hours. This schism between "what should be"
and "what is" has proven to be, shall we say, a major theme
in my life so far.

"Here, hold this cable, Lena. We're gonna do some close-ups on Sienna. I want to get a good shot of her stomach." Sal eagerly hoisted a tangle of wires onto my lap and went in for his shot. The stomach in question, which by all accounts did not look wide enough to actually contain vital organs, belonged to up-and-coming actress/model/singer/spokesperson and all around "it" girl, Sienna Skye.

At this particular moment, Ms. Sienna Skye was doing her very best to fan the flame of her generally agreed upon fabulousness. I watched her now as she preened for the camera to the delight and amazement of the crew. Of course, anything that she might think to do right now would very likely be deemed exquisite/otherworldly/magical, and just absolutely right. You see, this was Sienna Skye's moment.

"Guys, I'm going to go make a quick change. This tube top would look better in pink, don't you think?" Sienna chirped as Sal and the rest of the crew looked at her slack-jawed, their line of vision matching up exactly with the tube top in question. "Okay, I'll be right back." She hopped down from her perch and scampered off to her dressing room.

"All right," Sal tried to collect himself, "Nina, where are you? Nina?"

"Lena?" I asked.

"Uh, yeah, of course that's what I meant." Sal looked annoyed. "Listen, you're about Sienna's size. Get up there and stand in her place so we can fix the lighting."

"Sure," I said, noting the crew's palpable disappointment. "She's coming right back, you guys." They didn't seem comforted. It was true—I *was* about Sienna's size—only my chest was a few inches flatter, my skin was a few shades paler, and my hair was a few tones darker than her platinum locks. Essentially, I could be Sienna's "before" picture in a makeover story.

Sienna and I did have at least one thing in common, I thought to myself as I did my best impression of a hot young ingénue—Arch back! Suck in stomach! No, I didn't dream of a *Playboy* pictorial or my own line of lingerie, but just like Sienna, I had come to New York looking for something bigger than what I had left behind.

Mine was a tale as old as Dreiser and as new as *Felicity:* Small town girl moves to the big city to grab her slice of the pie and a little bit of glamour on the side. Her parents fear for her safety, she fears for her bank account, but most of all, she waits for her turn to come.

My life, I figured, could be divided into three rather distinct phases—BC, DC, and PC. Let me elaborate:

BC: As the letters imply, BC (Before college) was a dark, desolate time in my life's history. It encompassed a period of small-town ennui mixed with a difficult blend of adolescent angst and general alienation from my fellow peer group, a perplexing herd who expressed a troubling contentment with pep rallies and jobs at the mall. Overall impression—melancholic.

DC: During college. Known to some close friends as the "Greg" years in honor of my omnipresent boyfriend of the time, this period was marked by a perceived sense of liberation and freedom, which, upon reflection, was neither. The smell of boiling ramen and patchouli incense are key indicators of the DC era. Overall impression—naively happy.

PC: Post-college years. Otherwise known as the *Breakfast at Tiffany's* years or, more simply, as the present. PC is the time I've dreamed of my entire life, the moment when my life became my own, when everything was supposed to make sense. Yet somehow everything seemed more complicated than it ever had before. Overall impression—equal parts exciting and confusing with a sprinkle of adult-size fear for good measure.

A bit melodramatic? Perhaps. But then I'm convinced that just about everyone living in New York City feels they are currently starring in the movie of their own life, just a small step away from their own much-deserved "moment."

My cell phone rang. Sal rolled his eyes.

"Hello," I said.

"Hey, it's Nick."

I rolled *my* eyes.

"Why are you calling me?"

"Relax, darling. I'm finally getting around to picking up my canvases from your apartment and I can't find a few of my things."

Nick the painter. Long story short—we met at a gallery opening the previous summer. He wasn't textbook good-looking, but he had a certain way about him that made the whole greater than its parts—does that make sense? Olive skin, crooked nose and the fullest, ripest lips. Plus, he spoke Italian and could whip up a pencil sketch of my likeness (only prettier!) in a matter of moments. What else could a girl want?

And it was summer, when life sort of slips into that hazy mode of possibility and the idea of skipping work to frolic in the park with your smoky artist boyfriend seems romantic, not irresponsible.

Of course, winter came, the haze evaporated, and, alas, Nick's lips became horribly chapped. Love's languor was definitely lost. I had gone from being the enchanted muse to the broke patron. That phase lasted several painful more months until we had broken up officially. Now it was summer again, and I was single once more.

"So, do you know where my bottle of gin is?" he asked.

"I bought that gin."

"But you don't drink gin, love."

"Nick, I don't intend to drink it. I intend to use it to ignite the fire I will set if you're still in my apartment when I return. Cheers, darling." I snapped my phone shut.

"Jesus, Lena, you don't beat around the bush." Sal grinned at me through a mouth full of Doritos.

Okay, where was I before Nick so rudely interrupted me? Speaking of men, I should make one thing very clear—I'm most certainly not some vapid princess waiting for my handsome Prince Charming to save me. Please. I'm fully aware that the only way I'm going to get my ruby slippers any time soon is with an AmEx card and a couple weeks of overtime. Five years on my own in this city has toughened my shell and significantly toned down any lingering Pollyanna reflexes. But a girl's gotta dream, right?

Some days I imagine myself a boyish Annie Hall with my tweed pants and quirky hats, coyly befuddling and effortlessly stylish. Other days, I am the spunky young professional, the bright-eyed Mary Richards chasing her dream with a wink and a smile. And then, as you know, there are the parties with Marty, Joan and the rest.

"I hope you're getting all this down on the shot list…between phone calls, I mean," Nadine said to me in her distinctive half-joking-but-all-too-serious way that still manages to unnerve me after more than a year under her reign. Nadine (my "superior") and I, we just didn't quite "gel," to use one of her favorite terms.

She had the unfortunate habit of viewing her job (and thus mine) as something on par with the pioneering work of Edward R. Murrow. "Do not underestimate the power of journalism, Lena. It's our duty to tell the story, the whole story." She would say these aphorisms with a hushed, reverent tone. I didn't have the heart to tell her that our particular "news" program, an hour-long fluff parade called *Face to Face,* leaned more toward *Entertainment Tonight* than *World News Tonight.*

"You did finish asking her the preliminary questions, correct?" Nadine continued her inquisition. "You know we've got to prepare for the shopping segment." She said this in a way that managed to simultaneously convey both doubt that I had finished as well as disregard for any work that I might have actually done. If I wasn't so consumed by my unhealthy hatred of her, I might have marveled at the effort.

"Don't worry, Nadine. I grilled her while she was getting waxed this morning," I said as dryly as possible while hoping not to swerve accidentally over the line of contempt. Hiding my disgust had become a full-time job.

"That reminds me. Sienna's in the tanning booth right now for a touch-up. Remember to make sure she's out in ten minutes. Got it?" Nadine said, glancing down at her clipboard.

"Of course. We certainly wouldn't want a burnt Sienna!"

Nadine looked at me, expressionless. "Whatever, Sharpe," she said, and moved on to her next victim.

Believe me, it wasn't supposed to be like this. I wanted to be Murphy Brown, not Mary Hart, dammit. But here I was, laboring at the task of crafting the story of Ms. Sienna Skye, attempting to inject heroic purpose into her work as…well, as whatever it is that she does.

Of course, telling the "story" of Sienna Skye is a mind-numbing affair to be sure, but despite her endless references to the powers of yogilates and her colonic therapist, there is a story there, nonetheless.

You see, everyone has a story. This I know for certain. The trick is to weed out all of the standard, boring parts that muddle up the narrative. Of course, you might find it all very interesting—the childhood crushes, the "hilarious" high-school pranks, the first car and the last deadbeat boyfriend. It's your life, after all. Frankly, and I speak with some authority on the matter, no one else cares. Really. Better you realize that now, then on the winding-up side of a long-ass explanation of your last blind-date fiasco.

The trick is to find "the hook," that little kernel of experience where your life and other people caring about it intersect. I suppose you could call me a "hooker," which is actually a fitting alternate title for a TV producer, if I've ever heard one.

So, what's *my* story then? That's a question I don't find so easy to answer. Of course, I could easily do the *In Style* version. That's my job after all:

One might suspect the striking young woman seated before me to be an aspiring young model or perhaps the pretty young thing of some high-powered television executive. In fact, she's Lena Sharpe and she is fast becoming a power player in the world of television all on her own. At this moment, however, she's sitting with me in a charming café just down the street from her new Tribeca loft trying to decide between the egg-white omelette and the granola fruit plate. She looks glamorous, yet casual in slim Katayone Adeli pants and a crisp white Prada shirt (see how you can get Lena Sharpe's look on page 87!), and I can't help but notice the steady stream of gentlemen heading for the pay phone to sneak a look. She wears not a trace of makeup, but her skin appears virtually devoid of pores. ("Just a little soap and water. Nothing fancy. You can't worry too much about your beauty regime when you're field reporting in the Balkans!" she insisted earlier with a laugh.) "So, what would you like to know?" As Lena looks up from her menu and smiles brightly it becomes all too clear how this talented young reporter has won over an unprecedented Internet fan following as well as a coveted spot on People *magazine's 50 Most Beautiful People list....*

But what about the *60 Minutes* version? The Mike-Wallace-in-a-trench-coat-with-a-roving-camera-crew-and-a-running-litany-of-hard-hitting-questions version? Well, that was tougher. That required the truth and a lot of independent sources. What, in the end, would my story be? I kept turning the pages, past the twists and the turns and the disappointing moments, but I couldn't even find where my real story began.

chapter 2

"Hey, Lena, your phone's ringing," I heard Sal shouting at me.

Dammit, Nick, I thought, but then immediately relaxed when I saw the number.

"Lena. Meet me at the corner of Tenth and C at ten o'clock."

I could feel a wide smile spread across my face. It was Jake. And that meant that my night had taken a sudden U-turn for the better. You see what I mean? It can be as simple as that. Just one phone call, and everything changes. The city opens its arms and lets you play its secret games. Your moment could be just around the corner.

Of course, when I got to the corner, Jake wasn't there—not that I had really expected him to be. He wasn't the type to loiter for anyone.

I noticed a wobbly couple stumbling down the stairs of

an unmarked brownstone and I had a hunch that that was my intended destination. Once inside, I followed the echoes of a throbbing bass up a spiral staircase. The building was abandoned and police caution tape lay tangled in a mess of cinderblocks in the corner. If I didn't know Jake as well as I do (or if I hadn't lived in a building with a similar aesthetic for several years), I might have been more than a little afraid.

At the top of the stairs, a guy with hooded eyes and a vintage Gucci fedora leaned against the door.

"Who do you know?" He squinted at me critically. I appreciated his ability to remain haughty and suspicious of my cool factor despite his obvious stupor—quite a talent.

"Jake Dunn."

He glanced at the door in approval.

I rolled my eyes and entered. The place resembled a cross between a professor's library and an opium den. Couples lounged about in various configurations on the pillow-strewn floor. A midriff-bearing waif with a swan's neck balanced a tray of drinks with Hindi-painted hands. The scene was quintessential Jake. His coolness barometer was so precise he couldn't even hang out at bars anymore—they were too passé for him before they even opened to the general public. For the past year or so, he had taken to organizing "social spaces" (as he would call them) in abandoned apartments or buildings. That way, he could quickly change venues before "the wrong crowd" (read: anyone who lived—or would consider living—above Fourteenth Street) caught on. This wasn't a Jake event, but I could only assume it was the work of one of his acolytes.

Through the clouds of smoke, incense and various vapors of the illegal variety, I saw Jake's profile. Not surprisingly, he was the center of a swelling crowd.

How could I sum up Jake? Physically, he is tall and lean with dark wavy hair and deep blue eyes, which he knows how to use to full effect. More simply put, however, Jake is just cool. He knows it, I know it, and just about everyone who enters his orbit knows it, too.

Now don't assume he's just another snide hipster who chooses to define himself by his Alphabet City address and perpetual lack of employment. Jake, I long ago decided, sees it all for the game that it is—and he's the one to beat. The world is his to mock. I tell him he's so far ahead of the rest of us that he has to work to keep things interesting. He kind of likes that explanation.

So what, you may be wondering, does he see in me? Honestly, I'm still not quite sure. We shouldn't fit together, but somehow we just do.

I took a seat on a leopard-print chaise and quickly put on my studiously nonchalant "I'm alone at a party, but that means I'm independent, not dorky" face. A strung-out guy wearing entirely too much crushed velvet sat across from me. I began to ponder this point: Should a man ever wear crushed velvet? (I'm leaning toward no).

"Hey, sexy, you look thirsty." Jake slid his arm around my shoulder and handed me my drink. And yes, I do mean *my* drink. At the moment, it was Absolut Currant with cranberry juice. Jake has counseled me that a signature drink is a crucial element of one's personal style. I humor him (but of course it's Jake, so I also follow his lead).

"Oh…my…God." Jake fixed his eyes on a wide-eyed couple huddled at the door. "Honestly, *pressed khakis?* This place is dangerous. I shouldn't have lured you here."

"Don't worry about it. It was either this or face the artist colony that is my apartment right now."

"What? Nick the Dick?" he asked with bemusement. "Time to give that artist a chance to struggle."

Jake says that there is no such thing as a regretful relationship if you get a good story from it. With Nick, I had my starving-artist story all set, not to mention a nude oil painting of myself to drag out when I got really drunk.

"So, what are you doing later? There's a group of us going down to Ursula's to hear the latest self-styled, Dylan-esque knockoff. I'm sure it will be very earnest. Lots of corduroy."

"Ooh, I don't know. I don't want to run into that bartender I had the thing with. I still feel guilty about it and—"

"Guilty about what? About not calling him back after you had sex? You just did what every man does on a bimonthly basis—it's your right. You should feel proud in your womanhood. You're advancing the cause, Lena."

"Okay, you made your point."

"Besides he hasn't been there in months. Unless he morphed into a Latin lesbian with a spider tattoo on her stomach. She's the one working there now."

"Stranger things have happened," I joked, but couldn't help but feel relieved. Jake reached out for my hand and pulled me to my feet.

"Come to think of it, I don't think you have a tortured-musician story yet, do you?"

Ursula's was, and very likely would forever be, permanently stuck in the year 1993. It had all the elements of the grunge era down perfectly—the perpetually pot-smoky air, the basic beer and hard liquor, and, of course, the sullen alt girls and boys wearing every shade of faded denim and worn leather. The walls were covered with tattered flyers announcing the next march/benefit/protest rally. Personally, I couldn't imagine anyone here muster-ing the required energy to stand up straight, let alone rally against the Man, but it was a nice touch. And of course the music was predictably angst-ridden and mournful enough to make Eddie Vedder proud. I half expected to see Winona and Ethan hashing it out in a dark corner somewhere.

Jake had run into his girlfriend du jour, Miranda, at the door, so I went in search of a free table. I glanced over at the bar just to make sure Jake wasn't tricking me and was relieved to see the spider woman herself pouring a gener-ous drink for a Kim Deal look-alike.

I spotted a table next to the stage and motioned to Jake.

"Excellent work, Lena," Jake said as he approached the table.

"Hey Lena," Miranda said, looking past me.

It is often like this with Jake's girls. In the fruitless en-deavor of trying to get a firm grasp on Jake's roving affec-tions, I am the enemy. Of course, I always try to temper the situation by keeping my distance, making overt references to any current boyfriends, etc. But Jake usually throws a wrench into my efforts with a subtle touch to my face, an unnecessary story of "that time we had to spend the whole night in the car together." Yes, he loves the game.

"Oh, Lena, do you know if I left my cell phone at your apartment the other night?" Jake couldn't help smirking as Miranda visibly bristled. I half expected her perfect little head to spin off of her perfect little body.

"Oh, Jake, you're so funny," I started to say, but a pierc-ing noise erupted from the speaker that was, apparently, faced directly at us. So that's why the table was free.

"Maybe we should move," I mouthed to Jake. And for once, Miranda appeared to be on my side.

But before Jake could answer, the crowd rushed forward toward the stage, surrounding us as the band started in on their own variation of melodic melancholy. Oh well, at least I wouldn't have to make chitchat with Miranda.

I sipped my Guinness (ordering "my drink" in this place would be akin to donning a hot-pink boa) and settled in.

I had to admit the band was pretty good, and one of them, the bass player, caught my eye. I watched him bend over his instrument, his shaggy hair obscuring his (undoubtedly soulful) eyes. And like any perfectly sane person, I imagined how our life together would be.

Let's see—after going on the road for a few club tours and collecting a slew of zany stories as two young free spirits, "Ben" (a sensitive yet masculine name, I think) and I would settle down in a brightly painted Brooklyn apartment filled with funky art and mementos from our touring adventures. Our adorable toddler named…Coda, or something similarly eccentric, would be along soon enough. The house would be teeming with pets and plants, signifying our thriving fertility and life-breeding spirit. I'd attend PTA meetings wearing the latest frock from my collection of cutting-edge hand knits that I sold at my hip Williamsburg boutique (which was frequented by all the major fashion editors and constantly featured in the pages of underground European fashion magazines). At night, we'd laugh and talk as a family to the strains of Ben's latest composition for the film score he was working on. Coda would, of course, grow up to be a critically acclaimed filmmaker of socially and artistically progressive films, never failing to credit his parents for their loving and "creatively liberating upbringing" while giving interviews or delivering Academy Award acceptance speeches. It was so clear to me now.

And then, my beloved fantasy mate pushed his shaggy locks away from his eyes and…James?

I swiveled around so fast, I nearly spilled my beer. Jake looked at my fearful "Oh my God!" expression and instantly put the pieces together.

James the bartender, the one that Jake had promised me wouldn't be here tonight. He was a former quasi-flame whom I had abruptly and, I'm ashamed to say, not too gently let fall by the wayside when Nick and his lusty lips had hit the scene. I wanted to die.

I looked around at the swelling crowd. I was trapped. I kept my head turned toward Jake and prayed for the set to be over so I could make my frantic exit. Finally the last irritatingly soulful song was played.

Jake leaned over, sensing my panic. Miranda stiffened. *Jesus woman, this isn't about you!* I thought to myself. I wanted to throttle her little neck.

"Am I to assume that your evening is over?" he smiled. My panic impulses always amused him.

"Um, yes," I said sharply.

At that moment, I felt the brief stillness that you feel when a private exchange suddenly becomes public.

"Hey man, haven't seen you in a while." Jake had slipped into his low bass voice and Miranda ran her fingers through her hair. Clearly a heterosexual male was present. I turned to face the inevitable.

"James!" I tried—and failed—to sound surprised to see him.

"Hey, Lena, how's it going?"

"Oh, you know…" I said. Um no, he doesn't know, you moron, I thought to myself. You conveniently disappeared from his life nine months ago.

"Hope you enjoyed the show, glad you came by." Of

course, I'm sure what he really wanted to say was, *Glad you came tonight when I look totally hot and you're bloated with Guinness and playing third wheel to the Jake and Miranda show.*

"Oh, I did. You sounded great." Such conversational skills, no doubt he was thinking, *How did I let this one slip by?*

"Well, we're going to leave you two alone." Jake winked at me and guided Miranda over to the bar.

"I'm exhausted. Mind if I sit down then?" James asked.

"Oh, of course, please…sit."

So there we were, James and I.

"I didn't know you joined a band," I said, simply to distract my brain from concentrating on ways to kill Jake. "You were really good."

"Oh, thanks." He seemed genuinely flattered. No discernible bitterness—what was going on here?

"So, no more bartending, huh?"

"Oh no, had to grow up sooner or later and get a real job."

"Really? What're you doing?"

He looked around the room cautiously and whispered, "Investment banking."

We laughed conspiratorially.

"Can't say that word too loudly in this place." I smiled.

What the hell had I been thinking? I dropped sweet sincere James for Nick the Dick? I could feel my heart racing. It was fate—it must be. Nick was clearly the "temp," a harmless distraction until I was ready for James, otherwise known as "The One." Suddenly the chaos of my life made perfect, divine, joyous sense. We chatted some more—such a subtle, sophisticated sense of humor he had! And those sparkling brown eyes!

We would live in SoHo, no scratch that—the West Village, far west, near the Hudson. In a charming little town house with red shutters, a spiral staircase, and a beautiful garden in the back where I would grow herbs and James would barbecue. We'd take our time decorating the place together. There would be weekend trips to Vermont for antiquing, dinners at Tartine around the corner, summers at our beach house in Bellport (still fabulous, but not so "sceney"). After all, we were low-key, with an elegant understated sense of style. Definitely not one of those plastic Upper East Side couples dripping designer labels and angling for a Patrick McMullen shot in *Hamptons* magazine. No, James and I would be—

"Lena?" James was talking to me. For God's sake, I thought to myself, pay attention to the conversation or he's going to think you're totally spacey!

"Yes?" I said brightly.

"I want to introduce you to Madeleine."

Madeleine? My perfect Village town house had just been invaded by a willowy redhead with a Fendi bag. Home wrecker.

"Great to meet you, Lena." She slipped her hand around James's shoulder, and smiled at me warmly. Well, of course she was happy—she was dating my husband!

"Hey, I love your skirt," Madeleine said, as if she actually meant it. The sincerity of these two was really beginning to annoy me.

"Madeleine's a fashion designer. She just opened a shop on Crosby Street." Was he actually beaming with pride? It was beginning to make sense to me now—James had found "The One," a discovery that had left him so giddy that he had enough leftover glee to happily embrace any former flames with nothing but goodwill.

"Yeah," Madeleine said. "You should stop by sometime."

"Oh definitely," I said between gritted teeth. This needed to end—now. I found myself getting out of my chair and,

I'm sure, overexplaining how I really would love to chat more, but had to get home and…stick my head in the oven.

I elbowed my way through the crowd, searching for the sweet relief of an exit.

Once outside, I hailed a cab and headed home, mentally licking my wounds. Another night, another chance lost, I continued to pity myself. The city had won its hand.

The next morning, I had a ten-o'clock "progress meeting" with Nadine about the Sienna Skye segment. When I got to the conference room, however, I was surprised to find her already seated, chatting away with Chase Bolton.

Chase, or "Cheese," Bolton as he was more widely known, was a self-styled media mogul in waiting, a runt Rupert Murdoch if you will, who was biding his time answering phones for a VP until he had snagged his rightful corner office. Cheese had been my intern the previous summer, but after just one week of memorizing my Rolodex and vigilantly working his smarmy way up the ass of half the higher-ups, he had been whisked off to become an assistant in the executive suite.

"Hello, Lena," Nadine said, clearly disappointed that I had interrupted their conversation. Cheese gave me a cocky half smile and eyebrow-raise—a look that I'm sure he had rehearsed repeatedly in his bathroom mirror.

"Okay, so back to work," Nadine said, but of course offered no explanation as to why Chase was present. She looked at me briefly and then at Cheese, letting her gaze linger. He gave her his best half smile, but with a wink this time.

Oh…my…God. Were they flirting? The very idea made me sick to my stomach. Was Nadine *attracted* to sleazy Cheese? Sure, Nadine and I had our issues, but as a human being, as a *woman,* I wanted to grab her by her Claire's Boutique earrings and shake some sense into her—he's practically twelve years old! His feet barely graze the floor when he sits down! He wears his sweaters tucked in with pleated pants! He listens to Tony Robbins tapes! Don't do this!

"So," Nadine chirped in her blissful delusion. "The Skye segment is coming along pretty well…." I relaxed a little, sensing that at least this wasn't going to be one of her hourlong bitch sessions.

"And there's been a really interesting development." She paused dramatically. Nadine loved to pause dramatically.

"Sienna has agreed to let us film her—" another pause, and then in one breath "—while she shops for her People's Choice Awards dress." Nadine leaned back as if the weight of her announcement had left her exhausted. Cheese slammed his hand on his knee, in the most masculine form of giddy approval that he could muster.

I spoke up just to pierce their shared bubble of joy. "Great, so I'll start rewriting the lead and I'll notify the crew for the shoot."

Nadine turned to me with her silly grin still pasted on her face. "Oh, Lena actually there's been a slight change in the lineup." She loved to use sports talk. She thought it made her sassy.

I knew it. She was going to pawn off sleazy Cheese on me to help with the segment, so she could indulge her latent schoolgirl hang-ups. I started to formulate my diplomatic yet inarguable defense as to why this could never ever happen. And then…

"I'm putting Chase in the producer spot for the second half of the Skye segment." She shared a look with Cheese. I think the word "nausea" would have best summed up my feelings at this point.

"Nadine," I tried, in vain, to sound composed. "I've spent the last two months on this story and I really think it's best if I see it through." I was appalled at my sudden inability to argue and humiliated by the dawning realization that I was now groveling for permission to continue work on a Sienna Skye profile. This had to be some kind of professional nadir.

"Lena, it's part of my job to match my staff to their strengths and…" She glanced at the ceiling searching for just the right inflated language to explicate her lofty sense of professional mandate. She continued, "While you can be quite the worker bee, you're more of a serious Sally and this segment needs someone with the right…" Eyes to ceiling, searching, searching…

"Je ne sais pas!" Cheese exclaimed, now perched on the edge of his seat.

"Yes!" Nadine exhaled with a postcoitalesque finality.

"Quoi," I seethed.

"What?" Nadine asked, distracted. Her eyes were still locked on her little lover.

"Quoi! It's *Je ne sais QUOI!"*

The two of them looked at me blankly. And then back at each other.

At this point, I could distill only two coherent thoughts: Can a regular Bic pen puncture skin? And should I get these two a cigarette?

"Why don't you two switch research now, so we can get the ball rolling." Any further discussion was clearly over as far as she was concerned.

Chase handed me a hardcover book and a manila folder.

I was still confused. "What do you mean switch research?"

"You're going to be working on the project that Chase was doing." She looked down at her notes. "Colin Bates."

Now, I'd been to every agonizing editorial meeting under

Nadine's regime and not once had I heard mention of such a thing.

"I don't understand. Who's Colin Bates?"

"Well, he is a…" Nadine stalled.

"Writer," Chase pronounced triumphantly.

"Yes!" Nadine nodded. "He is a writer."

"I haven't even heard of this segment. When is it supposed to run?"

Nadine drummed her fingers on the table like she always did when she was dreaming up her next fib. She clasped her hands together decidedly. "Well, that hasn't been determined yet. It's really sort of a favor to one of the board members, I think. He's the author's uncle or some sort of thing." Which was another way of saying, it was a back-end segment that would be chopped to pieces and used to fill up the hour when the lead stories (like the Sienna Skye story!) left a few minutes of dead air.

"But don't worry, Chase has been working on this for some time. I'm sure it's practically finished, anyway." Nadine blushed. Chase beamed. I scowled.

chapter 3

Many New Yorkers viewed brunch as a shrewd social maneuver. They saw it as a neutral date to be offered in lieu of a more time-consuming commitment. It served as an agreeable meeting ground for sort-of friends, old acquaintances, out-of-towners, or new alliances—essentially, anyone who didn't quite clear the "let's go out Saturday night" bar.

For my friend Tess and me, however, Sunday brunch was now a tradition—a breach of its standing would be a first-degree offense to our friendship. Of course, we talked on the phone nearly every day, but nothing could replace our once-a-week heart-to-heart over scrambled eggs and strong coffee at Café Colonial.

I walked past the swirling line that had already begun to snake around the corner of Elizabeth Street and winked at Alberto (whose undying affection for Tess had won us a specially reserved table) as he stacked coffee cups behind the bar. Others may value their stock tips, their summer shares, or their courtside Knicks tickets, but I had come to cherish our table at Café Colonial to an unhealthy degree. I could not count how many perplexing guy issues, frustrating work fiascoes, and general I-feel-like-my-life-is-overwhelming-me-how-do-I-get-out-of-this-funk conversations I'd had at this very table. I suppose it's probably sacrilege to ascribe the wondrous catharsis of a religious experience to a vinyl seat and a plate of pancakes, but there you go—how else is an agnostic/lapsed protestant supposed to find enlightenment?

Tess was already seated. She looked immaculate as usual—her pale blond hair was gathered in a neat, low ponytail and her sea-green eyes gazed out the window. Tess always reminds me of a beautiful cat: serene, impeccably groomed and a little mysterious. She is the type of girl who uses words like "handsome" to describe men, can wear a string of pearls without a trace of irony, and hasn't owned a TV since she left home for boarding school. She has no problem sitting through the endless card games and executive dinners at the Metropolitan club with her current companion, Stanley. In fact, she has no problem with the name Stanley. Don't get me wrong, Tess is not a prude, far from it. She could sling one-liners and swill cocktails with the best of them. She just approaches her life from a different perspective than most (myself included). Sometimes, I can't help but think she understands me and my life so well because she is on a different plane altogether.

Tess is a two-kiss greeter. She has dated so many Europeans it has become second nature. I am strictly a one-cheek girl, but I leaned down and indulged her all the same. I slid into my spot next to the window and felt my body relax instantly.

"Sweetie, you look exhausted. I'm getting you a drink." Such endearments would normally annoy me—hon, honey, sweetheart—coming from anyone except my mother or my *amore,* but as with all things Tess—normal rules simply didn't apply.

She held up one delicate hand and I could almost hear Alberto snap to attention. Two bellinis appeared instantaneously.

"So, what matters of business do we need to cover this morning, my dear?" Tess was only half kidding. I knew she took these sessions as seriously as I did.

"Hey guys, sorry I'm late." Parker had appeared at our table, seemingly out of nowhere. "Had to get one last fight in with Brad while I was trying to get a cab," she said, struggling with her coat.

Tess gave me a look that, if expressed in words, would have said something like *Oh, I see that Parker has joined us for another cycle.* I responded in kind.

It had been at least three months since either Tess or I had heard from Parker (aside from the occasional group e-mail updating us on our bridesmaids' responsibilities—yes, she was marrying Brad) and much longer since she had made it to Sunday brunch. Of course, this kind of separation was not all that unusual after a certain age, when couples seemed to drift off into their own private biospheres. It's something a single girl must learn to accept in the way that she must accept painful blind dates, anxious mothers, and the sole responsibility of killing bugs and constructing bookshelves.

"Brad, I will talk about you if I damn well please...fuck you, too!"

Tess and I shared a confused look and then Tess remembered. "I always forget you wear that phone headset wherever you go. Good thing I didn't start laying into that no-good Brad like I usually do," Tess said mischievously. We could hear the muffled strains of an irate Brad through the earpiece. Parker smiled as she turned off her phone and removed her sunglasses. Her eyes were red and swollen.

I'd known Parker since college, but it seemed like she had been at least three different people since then. When we first met, she was deep in the throes of her party-girl persona—I think the first conversation we had took place as we both got sick in side-by-side stalls in a beer-soaked frat-house bathroom. Soon after, she gave up her hard-living ways and began her passionate quest to single-handedly launch the second women's lib movement. She grew out her hair, threw out her makeup, and even tried to adopt unisex pronouns in her speech. Then she met Brad.

Despite the transient nature of our friendship, she was the most direct link to my past life. She witnessed firsthand the Greg saga, in its glory and its tortured defeat. In fact, Parker, Brad, Greg and I had spent the better part of our undergraduate career in tandem. This shared history would perhaps be a source of comfort had it not meant that I would soon have to see Greg again at Parker and Brad's upcoming nuptials. Anyway, now she's a publicist and the professional world seems to suit her. She has a closet full of Gucci suits, wears dark-rimmed glasses without a prescription, and has cut her dark hair into a sleek pageboy. Even better, she can easily work herself up into a genuine tizzy over anything from the newest line of lip glosses to the latest PalmPilot upgrade.

"Well, I think we better start with you, Parker. What's going on?" Tess said, observing the damage.

Now, knowing Tess, this suggestion was very much intentional. Parker, when present, always went first. Why, you might be wondering, would the least reliable friend be allowed to go first? Very simple. Both Tess and I (and very likely even Parker) knew that she would quickly launch into a twenty-to-thirty minute monologue on the actual and tangential issues relating to her current crisis. She would insist vehemently (and completely unconvincingly) that this time she would cancel the wedding.

Meanwhile, Tess and I would simply nod or smile or frown, when appropriate, while we finished our breakfasts (French toast with lingonberry sauce for Tess; eggs Florentine with fruit salad for me). By the time she was finished, Parker would very likely have come to her own conclusions about her quandary or at least have exhausted herself by turning it inside out. Tess and I, now fully satiated, would have had enough time to properly caffeinate ourselves for our own respective rants.

I was polishing off my second bellini when I knew this was going to be a very specific type of Sunday affair. Every now and then, our brunch would extend well beyond the "meal" and turn into a messy, drunken, no-holds-barred, daylong event of relentless self-examination. And today was one of those days. It surely wouldn't be over until one of us had cried, argued, or made a spontaneous phone call to an angry ex or an unsuspecting crush.

I knew this because, against my better intentions, I could hear myself unraveling the tightest knots of minutiae about my failed relationship with Nick to the rapt attention of Parker, Tess and Wanda the cashier, who had joined the table after her shift was over.

"Honey," Tess said solemnly. She moved my head with her hands so that, had I not lost all ability to focus, I would be looking her in the eyes meaningfully. "You've got to stop romanticizing these boys."

"You're right," I said. And she was. It might seem strange to take such advice from someone who had gauzy scarves draped over every light fixture in her apartment, but I had to admit where men (or boys as she stubbornly insisted on calling them) were concerned, Tess had figured some things

out. She understood my problem. Hell, even Wanda understood my problem at this point.

"Sweetheart, here in New York he's an artist with a sexy
accent," Tess continued. "I'll bet you back home in Liver-
pool, he's just a short bloke with a coloring-book fixation."

"Wait." Parker put down her drink sharply and pulled
herself back from the table dramatically. Tess and I looked
at her expectantly.

"He's...*short?*" Parker looked dumbfounded. "You're getting this upset over a *short* guy?"

"I'm with Parker," Wanda said, picking at Parker's cold
French fries. "Case closed."

With that, glasses raised, we all burst into the gleeful
laughter of four drunk girls, gaily skewering the male
species for sport.

Oh, to bottle those moments of alcohol-induced clarity
before they hit the wall of sober confusion. Why couldn't
those moments last longer than the hangover?

I didn't make it back to my apartment until dusk. Not
entirely drunk, though certainly not sober, I was getting that
slightly apprehensive, sinking-stomach feeling I always got
as Sunday night descended. Plus, having spent the majority
of the day avoiding necessary errands, household chores and,
of course, work, this anxiety was laced with a heavy dose
of slothfulness.

Determined to at least portray the idea of productivity,
I turned on *This American Life,* straightened up my di-
sheveled living room and set up my computer. Whether I
actually did work was less important than the comforting
idea that I could, if necessary. I poured a tall glass of water
and set about the not-too-painful task of answering e-mail.
And then, this one caught my eye.

Hello Lena,
Chase Bolton gave me your name as the new contact person for my segment. Could you possibly let me know what's going on with it? It's been dragging on for some time now and I'm leaving town in a few days.
Thanks,
Colin Bates

I felt an inexplicable rage begin to well up inside me: Who does *he* think he is—writing me like this, pressuring *me* to get going on *"his"* segment? I found myself typing furiously.

Mr. Bates,
While I appreciate your predicament, I must also demand your patience. I was only recently handed this assignment and cannot be held responsible for the actions, or lack thereof, of my predecessor, Chase Bolton. I also do hope you're aware that this segment will be quite short and has no determined airdate.
Regards,
Lena Sharpe

With a haughty sniff, I sent it off. Who did he think he was? He was just some no-name writer telling *me* how to do my job. I looked down at the screen—a new message was blinking—it was from Colin Bates. Suddenly I began to feel painfully sober. I read nervously.

Hey Lena,
Not a problem. Just let me know when you can. And please, call me Colin.
—cb

What? I was beyond confused. Why was he playing this humble act?

I picked up his book, realizing that I hadn't even looked at it yet. It was plain and relatively thin, with the author's name printed inconspicuously below the title *My Indian Summer*. Oh God, I thought, no doubt it was the poor little rich boy's story of his fab summer vacation!

I flipped to the back—okay, so it had gotten some good reviews, even from the *Times* (but it wasn't Kakutani so it didn't count as much, I consoled myself). On the inside flap, there was a picture of a man's legs from the knees down. Underneath, it read: "A view of the author from the perspective of his dog, Emmylou. The two reside in Grafton, Vermont, where they enjoy playing Frisbee and taking long afternoon naps." I found myself smiling in spite of myself. I responded:

Colin,
Sorry for the terse message before. I was caught off guard when Chase handed over the story—just trying to get my bearings. Thanks for understanding.
Lena

Okay, so I wasn't playing hardball, but Jesus, after my work drama Friday and my brunch catharsis earlier that day, I was feeling pretty drained. Colin responded in moments. This was getting weird.

Lena,
Please—you're the one stuck with documenting my boring life! Anyway, I have to ask, what's the deal with Chase? I think he probably left me 20 messages about what I should wear for the sit-down interview. Strange one, no?
—cb

I was starting to like this guy. I wondered if he lived in a farmhouse. I could almost picture him lounging on a front-porch swing looking out at an apple orchard…no! I scolded myself. I had made a pact with myself—it was time to face reality. This was business. I sat up straight and began typing purposefully.

Colin,
If you wouldn't mind, I'll need you to provide me with a list of friends, family members, fellow writers, etc. that we can interview for background material. You can forward me the information via this e-mail address.
Lena

There. That wasn't so hard.

Lena,
Sure, no problem. Though, I have to say I feel a little silly getting all this attention. You're going to know everything about me and we've never met. I will get to meet you, won't I?
—cb

I thought for a moment about how active my imagination could be, how much trouble and heartache it had caused me over the years. And then gradually, imperceptibly, I found myself thinking about gingham tablecloths, jars of apple butter, and crickets at night. Dammit.

chapter 4

"Oh, Lena," Tess said wearily as she took a glass of champagne from a circulating waiter.

We sat down on a red velvet banquette and surveyed the crowd—a quintessential Parker production, more commonly known as a press party.

I didn't respond to Tess. I regretted having said anything to her at all about Colin and tried to look preoccupied with the scene around us, but that was almost futile. I had been to so many of these types of events, I was on a first-name basis with the waitstaff. It was always the same party with the same food—an assortment of tuna tartare on toast, mini quiches, and duck spring rolls. The cast of characters rarely changed—the usual mix of suit-wearing executives, a cluster of chain-smoking models, the stray B-list actor, and the odd club kid or two thrown in for the illusion of street cred.

"Hey, Lena, I'm sorry." Tess touched my arm gently. "It's just that I thought you were going to try to stop getting ahead of yourself. I don't want to see you get hurt again, you know?" Why did the avoidance of "getting hurt" always involve some other type of pain? I wondered.

"Tess, don't worry. I just think he's intriguing. He's a writer. He lives in the country. He has a golden retriever, for God's sake," I said. "He couldn't be more different than Nick."

"Well, that's a good start," she said.

"Besides, I haven't even *seen* him. It's fun just to daydream, you know?" I said lightly. In fact, I had not responded to Colin's last e-mail immediately for this very reason. The sheer ambiguity of our exchange allowed me countless fantastical projections about just who Colin Bates was and how our obvious connection would evolve. Could he have soulful gray-green eyes and a talent for making homemade pasta? Why of course! These questions (and my imagination's affirmative answers) could go on for days. I would sit at my desk happily sorting faxes or stapling Nadine's "memos" fueled by the giddy daydreams of Colin reading to me from his new manuscript as we slurped down freshly made gnocchi. Sigh.

"Just promise me you'll go slowly, okay?" Tess said, not giving up.

"Of course," I said, but she eyed me suspiciously. "I swear, Tess!" I said, and looked away.

Circles of guests performing their festive obligations collided around us. I noticed a woman wearing men's pinstripe pants and a tie wrapped around her chest like a bandeau top. A pencil-thin woman balanced a toddler on one hip and chatted on a cell phone—doing her best Jade Jagger-esque approximation of a bohemian parent. I spotted Parker expertly weaving her way through the crowd toward us, clipboard in hand, of course. She was in her element—a beautiful space, beautiful people and, most importantly, the position of authority to determine exactly who would be selected to enjoy it all. (I felt sure if Sleazy Cheese worked for Parker, he would be busy scrubbing floors in the back.)

"Thanks for coming, you guys—my agency friend flaked out on me again so we're a little short on the model quotient, but you guys help fill the space," she said brightly.

Tess and I shared a mental eye roll. It wasn't personal—Parker was like a choreographer and press events were her ballet. To her, Tess and I were the klutzy understudies that always came through when the prima donna ballerinas got sick—or, in this case, got last-minute bookings for a *Stuff* magazine photo shoot. Parker adjusted her headset and perched herself on a windowsill cluttered with party detritus.

"I'm also glad you're both here because I wanted to talk a little bit more about the dresses."

And we were trapped. Tess flagged the waiter for another round and we girded ourselves, secretly praying for a heated coat-check incident to carry Parker and her premarital monologues away. As if a sign from God, Tess's cell phone interrupted Parker's intense dissection of the difference between periwinkle and robin's-egg blue.

"Hey, Parker—I'm so sorry. I've really got to go," Tess announced, snapping her cell phone shut. "I'm going to go meet Stanley for a nightcap at the Knickerbocker." She gave me a heartfelt glance and with a kiss to each cheek she was gone.

"It's almost impossible to sit the two of you down long enough to go over anything." Parker looked annoyed.

"Actually, Parker, we haven't seen very much of *you* since the engagement."

"What?" She looked slightly offended. "I've been busy, Lena. Getting married is a full-time job. Brad and I have practically every weekend booked with appointments these days." It must be so taxing to explain these things to a hopelessly single person....

"So, are things better now between you two?"

"Of course," she said, without a hint of contemplation. Parker didn't contemplate. "We argue, that's all. It's a sign of passion, Lena." There were so many things she had to explain to me. Clearly my naiveté was exhausting her.

I wondered what it would be like to live inside Parker's head—to love your job and not question its "meaning" constantly, to see your future in front of you, down to the color scheme of your first child's (a boy—Bennett, or if it's a girl—Bethany) nursery. What was it like to imagine your husband and see an actual face that you knew—not some vague collection of traits that seemed "ideal" but weren't any more real than your childhood crush on Andy Gibb? Parker knew the rules and played the game. She knew what she wanted and she went after it with a zeal that sometimes scared me. She believed in the hierarchy of the world and comfortably, confidently, took her place within it. It was fun to make jokes about her new obsession with tulle and taffeta and her search for a good-looking reformed rabbi who wouldn't dwarf Brad, but at least she was living a real life, planning *real* events that were meaningful, not snidely standing by on the sidelines waiting for something, anything to happen.

"So, I don't know, Lena—I know it's a lot to ask, but would you mind?"

"Uh…" I had no idea what she was talking about.

"It's just that your color, as nice as it is, doesn't quite complement the overall theme." Parker raised her hands grandly and fluffed up the hair around my face, her eyes squinting critically.

"What color do you want it to be?" I asked.

"Brown with copper undertones." She smiled brightly.

"My hair *is* brown, Parker."

"Yes, but it has *golden* undertones."

Yes, I thought, Parker's world made sense to her. It did not, however, make sense to me.

"Parker!" One of her publicity plebes rushed to her side, his headset tangled in his overgelled hair. He blurted out some story about a nasty goody-bag tiff and Parker rose from her seat like a general facing the enemy.

I breathed a sigh of relief. Now that Tess was gone and dinner was taken care of (making a well-balanced meal out of finger food was a particularly good skill of mine), I figured it was time to call it a night. But then…

"Mind if I sit down?" A guy wearing a rumpled blue suit and a loose tie took over Parker's vacated seat. Lightning-quick mental assessment: Points added—broad shoulders, full head of hair. Points subtracted—ditch the cuff links and (oh no!) lose the class ring for God's sake.

Points to be determined—these events were usually all business, more about the illusion of a good time than the actual act—the subject's approach could indicate that he's an event novice, a naive young thing who has mistaken a publicity party for the pickup scene at the Cub Room.

"I'm Skip." Skip. This wasn't looking good. Point subtracted.

"I'm Lena—nice to meet you." Well, you have to be polite, after all.

"So, do you work for TCT?"

After a moment of confusion, I realized he was talking about the "star" of the party—some tech company's newest cell phone model (which Parker would gladly tell you both Brad Pitt and Gisele "absolutely swore by"). I imagined a walking phone with a feather boa and Gucci stilettos sauntering by.

"No, no…just a fan." I decided to joke with Skip. He looked confused.

"Yeah, so—I'm here with some friends from UBS."

Okay, I swear I'd misheard him when I said the following. "You work for UPS?"

"No." Skip looked genuinely offended. "UBS—the investment bank," he said, with a tone mixing both condescension and disdain. Did he know Nadine, I wondered? And what was so bad about UPS?

"So, what do you do at UBS?" I asked, in an attempt to ease his wounded ego.

"Well," he inhaled. And we were off. Let the discussion of "me, Skip" commence.

It always amazed me how some men would answer this question with such intense, highly unnecessary detail. I watched Skip's overbleached teeth bob up and down as he talked about internal messaging systems and transaction litigation. I noticed a mole, just under his nose. It had a long gray whisker just waiting to be plucked.

"So, me and the boys are just out to celebrate the deal."

And so you came to a phone party.

"I know the party planner and she got me in," he added.

Oh Lord, he was talking about Parker. I recoiled at the notion that Skip and I had other connections between us besides our mutual attendance at a phone party.

"So, what do you think of this tie?" His eyes gleamed. His eyes were gleaming over a tie. Bless him.

"Uh, it's great." How else do you answer that question?

"Got it down in Dallas when we were scouting out the service provider like I was telling you. Funny story, actually…"

Actually no, it would not be a funny story. Not at all, that much I was sure about. Why was Skip talking to me in the first place, I thought to myself while he droned on? He must, in some deep, dark recess of his beer-soaked, post-big-deal, three-martini-lunch state of mind, think there was a possibility that we had some level of compatibility?

He grabbed a chicken skewer from a passing tray. I looked at him and knew he was one of those guys who spread his legs out on the subway, taking up an extra seat. I watched him concentrate on his skewer, like an animal with his kill. I hated him right then. Intensely. I bet he played golf.

I really was being harsh. On some level I knew I was wrong and petty. Maybe, just maybe, Skip saw something that I wasn't able—wasn't ready—to see.

"Hey," Skip looked up from his skewer. Our eyes met. "Did I mention that I *really* like your hair?"

The next morning, as Andre dutifully put the finishing touches on my new cut, I mentally repented for my previous night's transgressions and made my usual resolution never to drink or smoke again, to go to the gym, reorganize my closet, and to be nicer to men like Skip in the future.

"Little bit different this time, Lena darling."

"New season, new me."

Andre winked at me approvingly in the mirror. I wish I could wink like that. Mental note: work on wink.

Not that I felt sorry for Skip—not in the least. Skip, in all his plain vanilla banality, was going to lead a perfectly pleasant, content life. After all, he fit into the world's design like a hand in a glove (preferably by Brooks Brothers, of course). He very likely laughed at sitcoms, enjoyed dinners at the Country Club, and thought corporate culture was good and natural. He probably wasn't even embarrassed to read *People* magazine in public. Despite myself, or perhaps as some sort of punishment for my previous rudeness, I couldn't stop myself from imagining our life together…

I would drive a Honda minivan—we had considered a Lexus SUV, but that really wasn't the place to put our money right now, what with the kids being small and the dog would tear it up anyway, so the minivan it would be. There would, of course, be a bumper sticker espousing our love for some sporting team or proudly trumpeting our honor-student kids. Our life would be a cheerful stew of organized events—PTA meetings, neighborhood board meetings, Little League games, homecoming games, bake sales, charity drives, 5K runs, winter carnivals and summer barbecues. I'd wear a bob and layers of loose-fitting clothing by Dana Buchman and Eileen Fisher. Natural fibers, earth tones and sensible shoes would enter my life. I would make casseroles. We would play bridge.

I couldn't continue. And I wondered if it was because, perhaps, that life didn't really seem as odious as I would like to imagine.

I exhaled audibly as I exited the salon, feeling safe in the knowledge that Andre—who was *at least* twenty times cooler and more stylish than myself—felt I had made a sound hair decision.

My cell phone rang. I swung my new tresses to the side and answered.

"Jesus, Lena, I *cannot* believe you!"

Parker. Here we go.

"Why? Of all people? Why did you have to single out Brad's best friend to perform your one-woman sarcasm revue?"

Skip was Brad's best friend? Of course.

"Look, Parker…" I decided to deal with her calmly.

"Sometimes, I just don't *get* you," she said, exasperated.

Even more positive affirmation, I thought happily. I was definitely feeling better.

"You do realize he will be walking you down the aisle, don't you?"

"What?" I do believe I screeched.

"Stop it, Lena. You're the only two that are unattached—you'll practically be spending the entire evening together. I thought it would be a good thing for you."

Yes, I thought, good like a colonoscopy is good for you.

"*What* do you have against nice guys, after all?"

Screw calmness. This was my moment.

"He called you a party planner," I said, waiting for the inevitable explosion.

There was silence. And then the brittle tap of Parker's manicured nails on her brushed metal desk. And then…

"That fucker."

At 9:58 p.m., I poured some Chardonnay into my favorite plastic cup and folded myself snugly on the couch with my laptop resting nicely on a stack of throw pillows. I wondered briefly if this was how Internet porn users approached their task, but pushed the thought out of my mind as quickly as possible.

At 10:06, a particularly inauspicious time I thought, I typed a message.

Colin,
Just happened to be online—are you?
Lena

I took a sip and waited. And waited. And then…

Lena,
Hey there. I've been sitting here staring at the same para-

graph on my computer for a solid hour. What's a more, ahem, literary word for "sticky"? Anyway, I could use some pleasant procrastination. What's up?
—cb

Interesting. He was approaching our online exchange as a welcome, almost expected—and appreciated—diversion. Subtle signs, but good ones. Still, must proceed cautiously. After all, I had made the initial overture.

Colin,
I know that you're loath to subject yourself to the grimy, swarming mass that is the modern-day media, but—alas—I am a working gal and I've got a pesky little deadline (not to mention a pit-bull of a boss)... Can we talk business?
Lena

I took another sip of wine and waited.

Lena,
You bring up an interesting point. Isn't the better question, this one: Why have you let yourself become a willing player in a liar's game? Lena, I'm concerned—help me understand.
—cb

Oh, he was good. I paused, considering my response.

Colin,
You are quite sly, but don't think I'll be distracted from my objective by the lure of dissecting my own story—it's not that interesting.
Lena

His response took an unbearably long time. I began my self-loathing monologue—*I'm so boring. Why am I assuming such familiarity? I'm just a big, big, big, big dork.* And then...

Lena,
So, how does one convince you to tell your story?
—cb

My heart leaped. He wanted to know my story? Mine? And then I panicked—I don't have a story! There is no story! I'd set him up for a story and I did not have one!

Lena,
I'm waiting...
—cb

The cursor blinked impatiently—or was it flirtatiously? He was not, I could tell, in the mood for business. Shouldn't I welcome this exchange? Yes, yes I should. I was sure of that. But how? Time was passing, I felt desperate. I started typing—something, anything.

Colin,
Nice try, but I think it's best if we concentrate on you right now, the next big literary thing that you are.
Lena

I was so lame, lame, lame, lame, lame. What was wrong with me?

Lena,
I don't think you think it has to be that way. What do you think?
—cb

Colin,
Hmm, let me think about it.
Lena

Lena,
But I'm bored with "me." Isn't that why we write, after all, to avoid the unrelenting burden of self?
—cb

Colin,
You are certainly quite the philosopher tonight. But, for the sake of sparing me the rancor of my superior, I must beg you to shoulder the "burden of self" for just a few moments…
Lena

Lena,
Excellent opening—thank you. Let's talk about this boss of yours. Explain this relationship.
—cb

    I didn't respond. I had lost control of the conversation. I didn't really want to talk about myself, but, on the other hand, did I really want him to stop? I was flattered by the idea that he wanted to know about me, but I was terrified that the sad truth of my answers would extinguish any further curiosity. I decided to be sarcastic, as usual.

Colin,
I couldn't begin to explain that relationship. Any attempt, however, might cure your tendency to procrastinate.
Lena

Lena,
Okay, new topic. What's your favorite time of day?
—cb

My favorite time of day? I paused, unsure how to re-spond. Now he was posing esoteric, soul-searching ques-tions. Jesus, couldn't we just talk about movies or something!

Colin,
Is this a trick question?
Lena

Lena,
No, just an innocent one.
—cb

Colin,
You tell me first.
Lena

Lena,
Dawn. Trite but true.
—cb

Colin,
Midnight.
Lena

Lena,
Why midnight?
—cb

Colin,
You first.
Lena

Lena,
Oh, you know—the world's asleep, the day is new, the streets

are empty, Hallmark card shit. And I can finally let my dog run around without a leash.
—cb

Colin,
Eloquent.
Lena

Lena,
Thanks. Your turn.
—cb

He had a way of unnerving me. I felt like I had to answer *his* questions. And well.

Colin,
Because it's the dividing line. It's the point between yesterday and tomorrow, between reasonably late and obscenely late. It separates the men from the boys, so to speak. Does that make sense?
Lena

What was I talking about? I had that feeling I got when I realized that I had said something intensely personal without meaning to.

Lena,
Are you a writer?
—cb

I didn't know what to say—or write. I was so embarrassed by my poetic declaration. He was a writer, not me.

Lena,
Hello? Are you there?
—cb

I exhaled and sat up straight...

Colin,
Don't be silly...I'm just a TV producer—that annoying person who's supposed to sum up your life in 9 minutes and 22 seconds. As such, it's my professional duty to remain impartial, objective, inscrutable. Now, start sharing.
Lena

He was trying to have a real conversation and I had blown it. He made me wait for his answer. Retribution?

Lena,
How am I to spill my innermost feelings to an "impartial, objective, inscrutable" listener? Hmm?
—cb

Good question.

The next day, Colin finally relented.

Lena,
I will boldly get this ball rolling, if for no other reason than to stop my publicist from leaving me threatening messages—I think I'm getting some insight into that boss of yours. Now, forgive my bluntness, but here is a list of the people who will likely (hopefully!) speak about me in unwavering, hyperbolic platitudes.
MOM (also known as "Libby Bates"): A no-brainer really. Should be very useful for teary, sentimental moments, if you so choose...
DR. ARTHUR LEEDY: Bespectacled, tweed-wearing professor who wisely spotted young Colin's burgeoning talent and took him under his esteemed albeit aged wing.

CALEB: Best friend since boarding school, like a brother, good for embarrassing but good-natured stories about youthful high jinks.
There. A perfectly embarrassing start. Please kindly refrain from undue mocking.
Yours,
Colin

I sat at my desk for nearly an hour before it sank in that my job—*my professional mandate*—was to examine the life of my most recent crush.

How fitting. I was, after all, a girl with a long and tortured crush history. They had started early and with a fierce intensity. The first one, as is so often the case, was the most painful. His name was Rodney and he loved Spider-Man. I spent endless recesses watching him play dodge ball, wishing unchildlike ill will on his opposing teammates. When he got a nosebleed during a lecture by the local fire chief, I cried quietly in the bathroom, hoping for his swift recovery. I wanted to know everything about him. I watched which foods he chose at lunch—sloppy joes or hot dogs, which ice cream he liked—Nutty Buddies with the occasional Fudgsicle for good measure. One day, he gave me a plastic Minnie Mouse ring on the playground. I thought it meant something. It, time cruelly proved, did not. Rodney moved away to Akron a year later. I looked it up on the map—it was three thumbs away. It might as well have been Africa, I remember thinking.

So, here I was, twenty years later, and not much had changed. Except this time, I held the key to the lock box of my dear crush's inner world—and I was *required* to look inside, inspect the contents thoroughly and report my findings. As difficult as it would be, I knew I had to quell my feelings and get serious. I might work for a show that considered a segment on Sienna Skye's Buddha collection to be hard-hitting news, but I was still a journalist, dammit!

I picked up the phone at least three times to begin my investigation, only to put it down swiftly when the realization of my task overwhelmed me. I needed coffee. That was it. I could be a different person when properly caffeinated—nothing would stand in my way. I was hyped-up, no-non-sense Lena after a particularly potent espresso.

I marched to the kitchen to search for my loot. I stopped short when I noticed a rim of spiky gelled hair peaking over the refrigerator door—it had to be Chase. The door closed. It was just me and the Cheese.

"Leeena. Heeey!"

He was holding a Stonyfield Farms yogurt, french vanilla. I felt strongly that it was not his. I always wondered who would steal their co-workers lunch out of the communal fridge. Cheese would. I had no doubt.

"Hi, Chase. Just getting some coffee."

"Midafternoon slump, huh?"

Could blood really boil? I pondered the thought.

"Uh, no Chase. I'm riding high on the adrenaline of my job."

"Oh right." He looked flustered. "Me, too." I'd challenged his own intensity. Cheese apparently had no capacity for sarcasm.

"We're just tweaking the Skye piece. It looks aaaaawe-some, I have to say."

He had to say that his piece looks "aaaaawesome." Perhaps because I shot all the footage and did all of the pre-interviews. Perhaps because I had all the visuals selected and edited. Perhaps because all Cheese had to do was position himself behind the editor with his arms crossed, and nod while Nadine called the few remaining shots.

"How's that thing you're working on?"

Physical violence seemed inevitable.

I said nothing. I eyed his yogurt. He shifted uncomfortably. I eyed his yogurt again and then looked into his beady, lying eyes, burrowing through his tinted contacts to pierce his dark, little soul. Yogurt, Cheese, yogurt, Cheese, yogurt, Cheese, yogurt, Cheese, yogurt, Cheese.

"Okay, well I've got to get back to the edit," he stammered, backing away. I waited.

"Hey, Chase."

He turned cautiously. I paused.

"Don't you want a spoon?" I let the words slither out slowly.

His mouth was slack, his eyes wide. He said nothing and scampered away like a roach caught by the kitchen lights.

I marched back to my desk, resolute. I didn't need coffee—I was running on rage. Call number one: Professor Leedy.

I punched the numbers as casually as if I were calling Tess. It rang. I waited.

"Hello?" An elderly man answered.

"Hello, Professor Leedy?"

"Speaking."

I could hear classical music in the background. I imagined he was working on a lecture, editing a book, formulating a new school of thought, while smoking a pipe of some sort.

"Hi, I'm Lena Sharpe. I'm working on a television profile of Colin Bates."

"Oh, yes, yes, dear—he told me you might call."

I loved Professor Leedy already. He was the sort of college professor that I was *supposed* to have had—not the endless stream of messy-haired grad students with bad breath,

trudging through their sixth Ph.D. year, working on disser-
tations about the role of identity and gender in twentieth-
century post-WWII Slovakian cinema.

I pictured Professor Leedy, settling back in his worn
leather chair, surrounded by richly hued mahogany furniture, plush Oriental rugs, and an eclectic array of classical
busts and collected artifacts from his travels throughout the
world. He would be reserved but warmhearted, pleasantly
rumpled but mentally disciplined. He would listen carefully,
speak infrequently, but counsel wisely. He would drink
bourbon and wear tweed.

"Colin, I can tell you," he began unprompted, "is a real
talent. Have you read his poetry?" He asked, sounding as if
he truly hoped I had.

"Well, no—I didn't realize he wrote poetry." I was
blushing.

"Oh, you must read it, Lena. Though I'm sure Colin
would be incensed if he knew I'd shown it to you! He's still
a young man trying to preserve his tough outer shell, after
all."

"Well, I'm afraid it's my job to chip away at that very
shell." I wasn't sure where my words were coming from, if
you must know.

"I suppose it is, my dear." He paused, raising one eyebrow
I felt sure. "I think you'll find it to be a rewarding task
should you be persistent."

Was Professor Leedy testing me? Could the wise, aged professor be sniffing out a potential match for his prized pro-
tégé? It was a ridiculous thought, but… I panicked—how
does one appeal to an octogenarian Milton scholar? What
would an octogenarian Milton scholar look for? Intelligence,
yes—I could string a sentence together, perhaps toss in a literary reference or two, sure. Problem was that I never found

myself to be less coherent and more ditzy than when I was trying to project an erudite image. And, let's be honest here, I was not in the daily habit of deconstructing classic literature—it just wasn't how my life was organized at the moment.

"So, it's done—I will send you my volume. I really think that it will help you get to the heart of, well, *his* heart." He chuckled lightly.

There, that wasn't so hard, was it? The next call, however, would not be as easy. There really was no way to prepare for this one. I cleared my throat and tried to detach myself from the bizarre nature of the task at hand. This is my job. This is my job. This is my job.

Libby Bates answered the phone herself. She sounded refined, elegant, educated. And tall. Definitely tall.

"Hi there." Hi there?

I looked down at my notes—yes, I had notes.

"This is Lena Sharpe. I'm an associate producer at the television show *Face to Face* and I'm calling about the profile of your son, Colin, that we're doing." I started to understand how a telemarketer must feel: *And, if you have a moment, I'd like to discuss your long-distance telephone service.*

"Oh yes, of course. Could you just hold on for one second?...Teresa, would you mind watching the stove for me for a moment. I'll need to take this call. Thank you."

I was a call she "needed to take"! I wondered what she was cooking. I was glad that she didn't expect Teresa to take care of *everything.*

"Yes, I'm so sorry. We're having some people over tonight, so it's a bit chaotic here." She said this in a way that seemed to convey that she didn't mind the chaos so very much.

"Oh, I'm sorry—I don't mean to interrupt. I can certainly call back at a better time."

"Oh no, don't be silly. I'm glad you called. I'm just so proud of Colin—I realize of course that that's not a shock, coming from his mother after all." She laughed. She did seem proud, but not in a boastful, "my child's talent is a reflection of my own" or "isn't it now obvious what a fabulous job I have done raising my child" way. Just genuine excitement and goodwill. Touching really.

"I was just calling to see if you might be willing to do a short interview for the piece—"

"I'm so sorry, Lena. One second." And then, "Teresa, would you mind letting Emmylou in—she's scratching at the door." Emmylou! *Colin's* Emmylou?! Yes, I was this excited over a dog.

"I know!" Libby Bates exclaimed suddenly. I wasn't sure if she was talking to Teresa, Emmylou or me.

"Why don't you come over tonight for the party and we can talk about it there?" She was pleased with her solution. I was speechless.

"Oh, well, of course," I stammered and then, worried that I seemed rude, I tried to be more emphatic. "Of course, I'd love to."

"Fantastic. We're at one-eighteen East Ninety-second. You should come by around eight or so. It's just a silly casual thing for the Central Park Children's Zoo."

"This is so kind of you, Mrs. Bates."

"My pleasure, darling. Really. See you soon!"

I hung up the phone—confused, nervous and excited. This was not in my notes.

chapter 5

I flung open my closet and glanced at the clock. I had exactly four and a half hours to reinvent myself as the perfect daughter-in-law designate. I knew what I needed to do.

"I need your help."

"Honey-bunny, what is it?" Jake said, sounding as if he'd just woken up. Or maybe he was drunk?

"I need you to come with me to Colin's mom's house tonight."

"Lena, sweetheart. Tell me you're not still fixated on this one, please."

"It's *not* a fixation," I said, irritated by the description. "It's a…it's, I don't have time to explain what it is. It's my job. Can you come with me or not?"

"Well…"

"Just—can you come? Say yes."

"I was planning on alphabetizing my CDs."

"Nice try, but we both know they're already alphabetized."

"Not by genre."

I said nothing.

"Seriously, I'm sorry, Lena—I have to watch Crumbcake tonight. She had some tests at the vet today and she's wearing one of those lovely doggie cones around her neck. It's a pathetic sight, really."

Crumbcake was Miranda's dog. Correction, "Gateau" was her dog; Crumbcake was what Jake had rechristened her. She was bony and loud, with a bracing bark that could sound both whiny and critical. In other words, she was Miranda.

"Bring her with you." I knew then that I was, legitimately and officially, panicked.

"But she hates you, Lena."

"True." He had a point.

"Plus, Miranda will find out and then I'll have to deal."

I imagined Crumbcake and Miranda having a furious and intense discussion of her trauma.

"I know, I'll ask Super Si to watch her," I said. Si was my super and on more occasions than I care to remember, I had called on him to chase cockroaches around my apartment, fish a necklace out of the drain, and perform various forms of spackling triage on my crumbling walls. I call him Super Si because he's a super and because, well, he's super. I tried to explain this to him once, but it didn't translate, like so many thoughts I had, when said out loud.

"God, Jake—for fuck's sake, get over here."

"Is there really a need to swear *and* use the Lord's name in vain? I think one or the other would suffice."

"Jake—it's *so* not the time."

"I know, I know. I'm sorry—I'll vespa right over." For the record, Jake did not have a Vespa, but he felt that he really *should* have one. No, he had a used ten-speed.

I felt calmer instantly. Jake's skill with a closet was akin to a natural chef's ability to transform saltines, ketchup and canned tuna into a sumptuous feast.

Exactly fifteen minutes later, Jake arrived. Head-to-toe Paul Smith. An irate Crumbcake accessory was the only thing that detracted from his perfection.

"You look…perfect," I said with a mixture of envy and admiration.

Jake, oh so modestly, made an exaggerated, Mark Vanderloo-esque turn.

"I really, really do—don't I?"

He was only half kidding.

"But there is one, reluctant concession." Jake pulled from his pocket a gleaming gray silk tie like a magician displaying his hidden string of scarves. Jake didn't *do* ties. I was touched. "Just in case."

"So, how casual is casual?" he asked as he made his way to the kitchen to deposit Crumbcake.

"Therein lies my predicament—I'm not sure."

"Do we have any clues? Indicators?"

"None," I responded solemnly. "She just said that it was a benefit for a children's zoo and that it was…casual."

A somber tone had overtaken us both. We could have been talking about global warming, missile treaties, or maybe the ethical consequences of human cloning.

"I see, so it's 'casual,' but not *casual*." He seemed to have gleaned a key piece of information.

"Maybe I should just call and ask?"

"Better you show up nude. Then she'll really know you're a neophyte."

"Do we have to resort to name-calling?"

"I don't think you're a neophyte—and all the better if you are. I'm channeling the mind-set of a sixty-year-old socialite, that's all." He shook off the thought with a chill.

"Okay, let's get down to business. Show me your little black dress."

I inhaled. I had dreaded this question. "I don't have one."

Jake paused. "You don't have a little black dress?"

"No."

"How can you *not* have a little black dress?"

"I know, I know—it's on my list of things that I really need to purchase." I was forlorn, distraught. "That and a spice rack."

Jake began to pace, rubbing his chin as he thought.

Jake, in the social sense, *was* the proverbial little black dress—he could go anywhere, accessorize accordingly and fit in flawlessly. He could chat up little old ladies in their Chanel gowns about the best places to winter their furs and the best spots to summer in Maine. Of course, he could charm the young debutantes with his lingering eyes and inherent hint of danger. Later he'd lose the tie and go share a joint in the kitchen with a chummy caterer and a gaggle of reverent Dalton boys. Parents were impressed, their kids were awed. They might not think he was "one of them," but they certainly wanted him to be.

"Okay, don't freak out, but this is what we're going to have to do."

"What?" I buried my face in my hands.

"You're going to wear Miranda's dress."

"Uh, no." I felt suddenly lucid.

"Lena, hear me out."

"Next idea."

"Don't argue with me, Lena. It's the only way." His words were grave.

"Why Miranda? I should call Tess."

"Won't work." His words were firm.

"Why? Tess has beautiful clothes."

"Of course she does and I would recommend her if this were a black-tie emergency. It's not."

True. Tess's collection did tip toward the uber-glamorous—lots of chiffon, and silk sheaths, etc. She never worried about silly things like "appropriate dress"—it was appropriate if she liked it, and she liked couture.

"But I don't want to be too casual, either."

"You won't be. And better to be too casual than overdressed."

"What?" I was confused. "Why?"

"Oh, Lena—these people can sniff out a wannabe in seconds. The worst thing you can do is try to look like you're…trying."

"Right."

"Put it to you this way. Consider the theater—who are the people that wear ties and prom dresses to the Wednesday matinee of *Annie Get Your Gun?*"

"I get it now."

Still, Miranda?

"I don't know, Jake. I can't think of a dress Miranda has that I would even *want* to wear."

"Tuleh."

Except that one. I inhaled sharply. I could feel my pulse quicken as I mentally pictured myself in Miranda's beautiful, beautiful dress. "Ready to go?"

"Great—this way I can steal back some of my CDs while we're at it."

Problem solved, we shared a moment of calm.

"What's that noise?"

Crumbcake. We rushed into the kitchen to find Miranda's precious morsel relieving herself on the kitchen floor. Was she smiling?

Jake grabbed a newspaper and placed it under Crumb-cake midstream.

"Lena, you may want to come look at this."

"Honestly, Jake, if there's one thing that I'm fairly certain I do not want to see, that's it."

"No, come here."

"What?" I looked over his shoulder. I saw a photo of a jeweled neck and the smeared inky face of an aging bottle-blonde. The caption read: "Libby Bates enjoys a drink at the Annual Spring Gala for the Southampton ASPCA."

"Cheers," Jake said with a laugh.

Half an hour and one stop to deposit a testy Crumbcake (and a thank-you box of Krispy Kremes) at Super Si's later, I found myself standing in front of Miranda's faux gilded full-length mirror.

"What is with this mirror? I am *not* this skinny."

"Stop it. I'm in no mood to feed your ego tonight." Jake was in a giddy trance as he gathered his long-lost CDs in one of Miranda's silk pillowcases.

I imagined Miranda standing in front of this mirror, modeling her latest cashmere cardigan or applying her ever-present lip gloss. The thought made me queasy.

I had the nervous feeling that I always got when I used to watch *Charlie's Angels* and one of the girls was sneaking into an office, stealing crucial, top-secret files with freshly manicured hands. This scene would be interspliced with footage of the suspect slowly ascending the stairs, on his way surely to discover her.

"Okay, we should get out of here. I'm nervous," I said.

"Relax—she's nowhere near here, I swear. It's her pedi-cure and Pilates night." Jake continued with his mission.

"Yeah, but I'm afraid she'll pick up our scent when she

comes back. Plus, all the chenille and shantung in here is making me congested, I think."

"Just let me finish here," Jake said. He was holding up a Luna CD. "Mine or hers?" He shrugged and stuffed it in his bag.

"Why do you have to do this now?" The thought just occurred to me.

"Because we'll probably break up this weekend." Jake said matter-of-factly.

"Probably? You haven't decided yet?"

"Nah, it depends on how ol' Crumbcake's tests come out. If the poor thing's really sick, I don't want to depress her even more. I'm a nice guy, right?"

"I abstain… So, what do you think?" I said, modeling Miranda's dress.

Jake turned and paused, but in a good way, I thought—not in a "how shall I say this gently way."

"Perfect."

"Really?" I was unconvinced.

He got up and stood in front of me. Was he going to ask me to dance? He pushed my hair behind my shoulders. "There."

I smiled. I felt something like excitement.

"Shall we?" Jake opened the door and we were off.

Excitement turned to nausea as the cab neared Ms. Libby Bates's elegant town house on a leafy stretch of Carnegie Hill.

"Well, this is very quaint—if you're into *vegetation*," Jake said, eying the block's prewar splendor with the detached ennui that only Jake could pull off convincingly.

Perhaps it should have set in earlier, but it was only at that moment that the reality of my current situation became clear: I was sitting in the back seat of a cab with another woman's boyfriend, in her dress no less, preparing to attend the party of the mother of my current crush (neither of whom I had yet met) in her home. Just another day in the life.

Moments later, we stood on Libby Bates's doorstep. The door swung open—and Jake and I were enveloped by the other half.

I felt the urge to swoon. Impeccably groomed guests wandered about the grand space. Plenty of wan smiles, the lilt of a distant French conversation, a lone voice rising to the climax of an amusing anecdote, followed quickly by the eruption of gentle laughter and knowing glances. All looked trim and rested and a disturbing proportion wore sherbet-colored cardigans draped with casual calculation around their newly bronzed shoulders (courtesy of Saint Barts, no doubt). "Look at that woman's brooch. It's gigantic," I said, overcome.

"Yes, but why is she eating a corn dog?" Jake said.

Sure enough, I looked over to find Brooke Astor's doppelganger daintily picking at her newfound delicacy with a dessert fork.

"That's strange, but it might explain why I saw a plate of something that looked a lot like s'mores when we walked in."

"Oh, I get it. It's peasant food as entertainment."

"Jake…"

"I can just hear the conversation, 'Oh, I know what would be so fun—commoner food!'"

"Jake, please don't get worked up."

"Lena, relax. I'm just kidding. Sort of." He slipped his arm around my shoulder.

"Stop it. We can't look like we're together."

"We are together, Lena."

"We're *here* together, but we are not together and when

you put your arm around me then it looks like we are, Jake."
I was worked up, officially.

Jake paused and rocked back on his heels. "So, who am I supposed to be—your walker?"

"Just be my associate producer."

"To your producer?"

"Yes."

"I don't carry subordination very well—you know that. It doesn't suit me."

"Really," I said dryly.

"And I'm dressed much more like an executive producer. In fact we both are. We blow this crowd out of the water, I'll tell you that right now." He rubbed his shoulder against mine playfully.

Jake *had* done his job admirably—we managed to fit in but still stand out, if you follow me. The Upper East Side casual dress code was in full effect—men wore open shirts sans jackets. Michael Kors made a strong showing among the women, though Prada and Escada didn't disappoint. I wondered which one "she" was amidst it all, and realized she could have passed by already—after all, we'd never met.

"Lena?" I felt a gentle hand on my arm and turned to see a gigantic sapphire nested on an impeccably maintained hand. I blinked back the glare and followed a trail of jewels up to the smiling face of…

"Libby Bates. So glad you could come, Lena."

Okay, I suppose we didn't blend quite as well as I had imagined.

"My pleasure." I felt a fleeting instinct to curtsy.

"This was my dear friend Delia's idea, I'm afraid." Libby waved her bejeweled arm around toward nothing in particular. At that moment, I noticed a dunking booth and an aimless clown. "It's a little silly really. It's supposed to look like a country fair. Or is it a carnival? Something like that." The decidedly gingham-esque print of Ms. Bates's Carolina Hererra skirt betrayed her professed embarrassment, however.

"Oh no! We were just talking about how fun it all seems. This is Jake, by the way."

"Yes, hello. Jake Jennings."

"Hi there, Jake. Pleasure to meet you."

"Yes, Jake's my…"

"I'm Lena's intrepid assistant."

"Pleasure."

I marveled at their seamless interaction. A gift.

"Well, you two should enjoy yourselves—I'm going to make sure things are running smoothly and we can talk later." And she was off.

"Jake Jennings?"

"Yeah, has a ring, don't you think? Better than Jake *Brokaw*."

"This is really too much to take in." Jake was spying a cluster of Blaine Trump types as they buried their taut faces into masses of pink and blue cotton candy. One plaid-wearing playboy with a pink oxford opened just down to there proudly presented his paramour with a freshly frozen Charleston Chew.

"I'm going to start a class war right now. Lena, back me up here!"

"Oh, Jake, it's not so bad. Don't be a snob toward snobs," I said, even though I kind of saw his point.

"You may be right. Excuse me one second, I just spotted a debutante in distress." With that, Jake made a beeline toward a sweet young thing searching for her Cracker Jack prize. I guess a truce had been forged.

I decided to make my way through the house, taking in the details. The furniture was beautiful but not precious—it was made for living, for raising a family, for active hands and feet. Vibrant, exotic paintings, antique furniture, objets d'art, lots of terraces with lush, fertile plants spilling out from large iron pots.

And then there was the staircase. It made no apologies for its grandeur, no concession for its opulence. It was simply awe inspiring—deep marble steps winding their way up to the next level guided by a carved wooden railing.

Yes, they were beautiful stairs. In fact, it just seemed natural to climb them—imperative, really. So I did. From the top, I paused to watch the frivolity below. There were more people there than I thought, tucked away in hidden corners, trailing out of various corridors. I noticed for the first time that there was music playing.

I felt comfortable from my new vantage point, so comfortable that I saw no harm in exploring the second floor just a bit more. How could I not? I was an investigative journalist, wasn't I? It was time to do some fieldwork, that's all. "Politeness" and "social boundaries" were for ordinary party guests. I was liberated from that restraint—I was doing my job.

One by one, I toured the successive bedrooms. Lots of muted shades of taupe, punctuated by a simple silk pillow or a cashmere throw here and there—every surface seemed elegant and right.

I arrived at the last room. It had to be his. I felt a gravitational pull. Pros vs cons filled my head. My bullshit rationalizations aside, I knew that I would most certainly have crossed an unhealthy barrier if I were to go into my crush's childhood room. Countering this unappealing argument was the very real sense that I might not get this opportunity again. What to do, what to do—my mind wrestled with this question as I pushed opened the door. It creaked stubbornly. I slipped inside. Where to start? I would not touch or open anything—what was the harm in *standing* in his room for a few minutes. Emboldened, I made my way in.

The plush carpeting enveloped my heels, and I caught my balance on a mahogany nightstand. Okay, so I touched one thing! The room had that familiar, time-warp feeling common to childhood bedrooms—at once intensely personal yet somehow universal in its depiction of a person's evolution toward maturity. It could have been my room, I thought—had I been a boy, a child of wealth and an avid collector of model airplanes.

I eyed a cluster of framed pictures on a nearby bureau. Colin, I realized, had been a beautiful child, I thought to myself without a pinch of bias. Unfortunately, most of the pictures around did not have him in them, of course, which in theory was a reassuring sign (would I like someone who had pictures of himself around?). I was still left wondering what he looked like now.

I stopped. At first, all I could hear was the unmistakable rhythm of flirtation—the deep bass followed by the obligatory high-pitched giggle.

"I noticed you the second you walked in."

"You did not!"

Forget Miranda's apartment. *This* was my Charlie's Angels moment. I needed to hide, but where? Of all things, why didn't Colin have his own bathroom?

The door creaked. I froze.

"Lena?"

Nick stood before me wearing a waiter's uniform. A drunk young wisp of a thing was draped on one arm like a wet towel.

This, I had not expected.

"What are you doing here?" He looked as shocked as I felt.

I thought for a moment, realizing that I no idea how to answer that question even if I intended to lie.

"What are *you* doing here?"

"I'm working."

"I can see that. You've always been such a dutiful worker." I glanced at Tiffany or Britney or whomever it was he had found himself with this time. Had it really been only a matter of months since I was the giggling idiot fooled by Nick's so-called charms?

"Look, you haven't answered my question." He was on to me and we both knew it. He had that smug, self-satisfied smirk that meant he might not know the details, but he knew I'd been caught and he was enjoying it. The drunk waif managed to extract herself from Nick's torso and flopped herself onto Colin's bed. The mattress sighed.

"I'm a guest at this party." I felt stupid saying this, even to Nick. So I continued, "I'm doing a piece on the host's son. He's a hugely talented writer." At this point, the truth was the only thing that didn't sound ridiculous.

"Oh, I see," Nick said.

Why was he making me feel uncomfortable?

"Don't you have some corn dogs to serve or something?"

"Oh, oh, oh!" The drunken waif rose to her knees on the bed. "Corn dogs are divine." And then she collapsed again.

"I'm a bartender here, Lena. So you know."

Oh, he was so not a *real* bartender—pouring champagne spritzers and Shirley Temples for this crowd was one rung above Isaac on *The Love Boat*.

"Look, I've got to go." I didn't want to leave these two in Colin's childhood bedroom to fornicate, but I was beginning to realize that the only thing worse than being found in Colin's room alone was to be found there with Nick and his little tart.

I raced down the stairs, a little too fast. I saw Jake at the center of a swell of socialites. His shirt sleeves were rolled up and he was nursing a beer, straight from the bottle. I waved my arm—this carnival was leaving town.

"Darling." I heard Libby Bates's voice behind me. Oh God, Oh God, Oh God, she saw me in her son's room. She heard me with Nick. She can't believe what a reprehensible young woman I am. She's going to tell Colin. Hell, she'll probably call *The Times*—this woman *knows* people. I wanted to die. I wanted to die.

"Lena."

"Oh, hello!" I turned and did my best impression of a relaxed, perfectly innocent party guest.

"I've been looking for you and Jake everywhere—I was afraid you had gotten sick of all the nonsense."

You didn't look in your son's room though, did you?

"Oh, I'm sorry, I was just admiring your home." That was true, sort of.

"Well, if you're up to it, I wondered if you wanted to talk about Colin's interview."

"Sure thing!" Jake said from behind me. The intrepid assistant had returned, slightly buzzed, his ego flying high.

"Great—let's go upstairs where it's quieter," Libby Bates offered.

"Oh, yes. I'd love to see the rest of your home," Jake said, clueless of my previous sojourn.

We made our way up the stairs—I could see the imprints of my own footsteps from before etched in the freshly vacuumed carpet. And I could smell Nick's cheap cologne.

"Have a seat." We arranged ourselves in the front sitting

room—or more descriptively—two doors down from the scene of the crime.

"Now, where should we start?"

Everyone was looking at me, and I didn't feel capable of stringing a sentence together, much less conducting a meeting.

"Well, it's very simple. We need to interview you in order to get to the private, more personal side of your son's life," Jake said, sensing my hesitation.

"Yes, we won't take up much of your time—it shouldn't last more than an hour for the whole process," I added meekly.

"Oh, don't worry—I could talk about Colin all day—I just don't think he'd want me to!"

"Great to hear. So, let's just go through some preliminary questions. It shouldn't take too long."

"Uh, Jake, I don't think that—"

"Oh, that's fine—not a problem at all." Libby Bates looked excited.

"Well, first off—tell me about your relationship with Colin. How he was as a child? Things like that."

Okay, maybe this would be fine.

"Well, he was always reading from the beginning, anything he could get his hands on. But not always what his teachers wanted him to read." She laughed. We took her lead and laughed, as well.

I interrupted the hilarity. "Tell me, if you don't mind, Mrs. Bates, when did he start writing on his own?" I had my bearings now. I was in control.

"Oh, very early. I would read him a bedtime story and he would make up the ending. Before long he would cross out the final paragraphs of books and write his own. My favorite was 'Clifford—the small purple dog!'"

We all laughed again.

"When did you know he was serious about writing as a career?" I wondered if she realized how generic these questions were.

"Well, it was more of a feeling of the inevitable, you know. Much to his father's chagrin. He wanted another lawyer in the family." She rolled her eyes again.

And we laughed again. It was expected at this point.

"All of his brothers went the traditional route, but not Colin. He was always an 'artist.' His brothers used to sneak out to bars, but Colin and his friends used to sneak out to go to readings!" This time, Jake rolled his eyes while Libby and I laughed.

"Tell me about his friends."

"Well, there's Caleb—that's his best friend. Wonderful person, but perhaps a bit…misguided you know. He's still finding himself, or what have you."

Jake was nodding now, scribbling "notes" in his notebook—yes, he had thought to bring a notebook.

"And his girlfriends?" Jake asked without looking up. He said the words as if he were reading down a checklist of obvious questions.

Libby Bates paused. I blushed. Jake scribbled.

I imagined she was thinking one or all of the following:

a) I understand now that you are both psychopaths.

b) You need to leave my home immediately.

c) I will call Colin now and tell him the truth about you.

"Oh, I don't think he's found the right one yet. He had quite a serious one back in high school, but I guess…" She trailed off.

She guessed what?

"You guess what?" Jake asked. Thank you, Jake.

"Oh, now there I go. I just think he hasn't found the right woman yet, that's all."

"Would you say he has a fear of commitment?" Jake was fearless.

Oh God, this was weird.

"Oh, I, well…" Libby Bates was confused.

"We're just trying to get a valid profile in order to find our angle on the story." Jake said this so assuredly and matter-of-factly that even I believed him (sort of).

"Oh, of course, of course." She nodded. "What I meant was that he always gets so involved in his writing that he can't always be involved in a serious relationship."

"Is he involved right now?" Jake's tone was so serious he could have been asking, *Is he having chest pains?*

"Oh." She thought for a moment. "No, not that I know of."

Shew. Mission accomplished. It was time to go.

"What would you say—" Jake began his question. He looked up at the ceiling, rubbed his chin, and searched for the right words "—he's looking for in a woman?"

"Mrs. Bates," I interjected before that question had fully registered, I hoped. "Thank you so much. I don't want to get too much information before the official interview. Want to keep it fresh, after all!"

"Oh, I hope I didn't bore you too much."

"No, not at all," Jake and I said in unison.

"I'll be in touch soon to set up the details for the shoot."

"Great. Maybe we can have it on the veranda or perhaps in front of the Matisse." She was thinking out loud. Her event-planning mode had been activated and I felt reasonably confident that she wouldn't dwell on our conversation.

"You really have been a tremendous help, Mrs. Bates. I hope we weren't too much of a bother to you this evening."

"Not at all, dear. Oh, maybe we could do it here in front of Colin's self-portrait."

"That's a lovely painting." I heard Nick's slimy voice. He stood at the top of the stairs, positioning himself as if he'd just ascended. His clothes were neat, too neat. Liar.

"Why, thank you—my son painted it."

"My, he's a painter *and* a writer?"

"You're familiar with Colin's work?" Libby Bates smiled brightly at Nick. I wanted to vomit.

"I've just recently heard some very interesting things about him, yes." Nick looked directly at me.

"Oh, do you two know each other?"

Nick inhaled. Jake stepped forward.

"Yes, we do. Back at Collegiate."

Nick retreated. He had been scared of Jake ever since they first met.

"That's right. Well I just wanted to say hello. I'd better get back to the bar." Nick said this as he started down the stairs.

"Poor guy, he's had a rough patch since school." Jake waited a beat. "I'd watch your silverware."

Once outside, Jake and I walked briskly in silence for a couple of blocks. When we reached Third Avenue, it felt safe to talk.

"I should not have gone there. I'm so embarrassed." Reality was setting in for me the farther away we got from the scene of the crime.

"What? You were fine."

"I so wasn't." I snapped back, but I was glad he had said it, anyway.

"Lena, Libby Bates doesn't have a clue about you and Nick."

"I was in Colin's bedroom when I ran into him," I confessed.

"The two of you were alone in Colin's bedroom?" He seemed to be more intrigued than concerned.

"Yes, with a drunk blonde."

"Wait, the one with the glitter top?"

"That's the one."

"Dammit. I was chatting her up earlier. Real nice girl."

I rolled my eyes.

"Oh God, Jake. We shouldn't have gone there tonight," I said, feeling suddenly serious.

"What do you mean?" Jake wasn't following.

"I mean it wasn't ethical. I'm still a journalist, kind of," I said.

"What did you do wrong? You had a conversation with his mom. It happened to be during a party."

"Right, and the part where I snuck into his room?"

"So? You got lost looking for the bathroom. It happens," Jake said, perfectly comfortable with his explanation.

"I don't know, Jake." I wasn't convinced. A crush was one thing. Trespassing was another.

"Oh, whatever." Jake was impatient now. "We crashed a corny zoo fund-raiser. No harm done, okay?" Jake said, putting an arm around my shoulder. He always had a way of calming me down.

"Yeah, no harm done, except Mrs. Bates thinks I'm a complete weirdo!" I said.

"Lena," Jake paused. "You shouldn't be so nervous about making a good impression on some guy's mother. I think it's virtually impossible for you to make a bad impression, in fact."

"Said my best friend thoughtfully," I laughed.

"Stop it, I'm serious."

"You're sweet, Jake."

"I can't believe old Nick was there." Jake seemed genuinely amused by my turn of bad luck. "I still can't believe you guys dated."

"Me neither. I'm trying to forget."

We stopped at a traffic light and I turned to Jake.

"I really appreciate your help tonight. You saved me in there."

"Aw, stop it." Jake waved me off. "You don't need me."

"You're my knight in shining armor," I teased him.

"I am?" He considered the idea for a minute. "Well, in that case, I better make sure you get home safely." With that, he picked me up and hoisted me over his shoulder. I was laughing so hard, I couldn't resist, and we were halfway down the block before I could convince him to let me down. Jake loved to make a scene.

"I'm dying for a drink. Not that watered-down cocktail-party shit, you know," Jake said.

"I know." I smiled to myself, thinking of Nick pouring highballs for the society set. "Let's go get a real drink."

When I got home, the stillness of my apartment overwhelmed me. After a night out, it always took me a few moments to readjust to the quiet. Alone again.

The phone rang.

"Hello."

"Okay, tell me you're watching *Savannah, the E! True Hollywood Story.*"

"I'm going to bed, Jake."

"Lena, this is gripping television—Savannah just wrecked her prized white Corvette after a coke binge. She's on the brink."

"Jake, I'm really tired…"

"Lena, she's not just a porn star—she's a young girl caught in the grips of the wicked Hollywood machine."

"I'll call you tomorrow, Jake."

"All right, sweet dreams, pumpkin."

I smiled in spite of myself.

I had just stepped into the shower when the phone rang again. Jake must have had another revelatory Savannah moment.

But later when I picked up the message, it wasn't Jake—the tone was low and even. It was a man.

I tracked water over the hardwood floor, giving my opposite neighbor another performance in my daily striptease revue. With one wet finger, I pressed Play.

"Hey, um, it's Colin—Colin Bates—" deep-throated laughter "—I'm sorry for calling so late, but I was planning on being in the city Friday and was hoping we could meet up—" and then quickly "—to talk about the book, I mean."

In moments, I had the message memorized. The pause, the beautiful, wondrous, meaningful pause…this was huge, this could last me for days, three Nadine meetings at least. I shed my towel, twirling for my audience, and floated to bed.

chapter 6

"I think we should meet for a drink. That's innocent enough, right?"

"Lena…"

"I wonder if he likes sake—there's that cool place on Ninth Street."

"Ooh, I know that place. Very cool," Parker chimed in.

"Don't encourage her!" Tess scolded.

"Tess, have you ever thought maybe it would be a *good* idea to encourage me, every now and then."

"Yes, but…"

"No buts…I'm on my lunch hour. I don't have time for buts."

"Who are you kidding? You don't get a lunch hour," Parker corrected me.

"Don't remind me. Nadine thinks I'm at the dentist again. I had to do research on gum disease to throw her off the trail this time."

"Can we just order now? I'm starving." Parker tended toward hypoglycemia, and let everyone know it.

"Yes, but—" Tess wasn't finished.

"No buts!" Parker and I replied in unison.

"Just let me say this and then I'll shut up. You don't even know if you like him yet. Don't get ahead of yourself."

"You tell her that every week," Parker remarked. "And we *know* she likes him. That one's not hard."

I looked at Parker askance. She seemed so certain.

"What do you think about all this, Parker?" I had never thought to ask her opinion. Now I was curious.

"There are three things a girl needs to ask herself about a new guy," she replied, not missing a beat. "I call it the AHI principle."

I, and I think even Tess, moved in closer.

"Age—is he older? Height—is he taller? Income—does he currently make more, or have the imminent potential to make more money than you?"

"That's so—" Tess began.

"Clinical." I finished for her.

"That's reality, girls. Men want it that way. Women want it that way. It's just that no one wants to say it out loud." She heaved a sigh, clearly annoyed by the burden of being the one woman who had figured it all out. "After those three questions are taken care of, any relationship can be made to work." She picked up her menu, fully content with her view of the world.

"Okay, I'm sorry, but that's insane, Parker," I said.

"What's so insane about it?"

"Uh, where do I start? Men and women are not that …interchangeable. You can't just match people up by their stats." I looked at Tess for backup, but clearly she was intent on staying neutral.

"You don't think so?" Parker said.

"I can't believe you think they are!"

"Lena, do you ever read the Sunday *Times* wedding announcements?"

"Of course."

"Have you ever noticed that a striking number of listings resemble the following couple—'Man, 36, investment banker. Woman, 27, elementary school teacher.'"

"Your point?"

"And how often do you see this listing: 'Man, 27, elementary school teacher. Woman, 36, investment banker'?"

"That doesn't prove anything," I said dryly.

"I know you think it's cynical, Lena, but it's just reality. You'll be so much happier when you accept it."

"Right, well if I had taken your advice, Parker, I'd probably be married to Greg right now!" I laughed at the thought of it.

"And what would be so wrong with that?"

"Just about everything," I shot back.

Greg. Greg was the past, pre-New York, prerevolutionary Lena Sharpe. If my life was Berlin, Greg was the Wall. Perhaps I was being dramatic. The fact of the matter is that we had dated. During college, I hadn't had many relationships beyond a drunken hookup or two. Greg was, at the time, a revelation. A living, breathing, heterosexual male who wanted to have sex with me and talk to me in the mornings. He seemed, at the time, to be a natural, comfortable, perhaps larger-boned extension of myself. It seemed bizarre now to have been so intimate with someone, to have shared food, clothing, bodily fluids, and shelf space and then completely lose touch, vanish from each other's lives completely. There was a time when I wondered if Greg was my destiny and yet now, I couldn't even imagine what he looked like.

"Well, I guess we would make sense together if I followed the AHI principle, but that's about it," I kidded. Tess snickered.

"Laugh if you will, but you'll understand my way of thinking one of these days," Parker chided us. "Oh, and I almost forgot." She slammed down her menu, alarmed at her omission. "STP ratio is also very important."

"STP?" Tess asked.

"Yes, shoe-to-pant ratio. You *must* find a man who can pick a pair of pants that fall just right, you know? *Very* important."

Colin and I would meet at Le Gamin at seven o'clock— just a casual chat over coffee at a little café conveniently located near my apartment. I had wrestled over the venue for hours. First it was to be the Hudson (too flashy for a first meeting I decided), then it was Pravda (too Euro-trashy for someone returning from the New England countryside), and then finally (with much prompting from Tess) I decided to downgrade. Le Gamin was my Saturday-afternoon hangout, perfectly suited for lounging, smoking and elevated conversation. Plus, I had perfected just enough French to banter with Olivier, the counter guy, and one couldn't dismiss such opportunities to impress one's date with calculated displays of sophistication.

I had just spent a busy afternoon at the office volleying e-mails with Tess. She had, not surprisingly, tried to talk me down from the admittedly lofty supposition that I was, in fact, about to meet my soul mate and life partner.

In fact, I had almost entirely convinced myself that I nursed only the mildest curiosity about Colin Bates by day's end. I even managed to hold on to this idea as I left work early to get a quick blowout at Bumble & Bumble, ran home to change my clothes (and then change them again) and finally, dab on my new M.A.C. lipstick (Viva Glam!) that I had just happened to purchase that day after I (oh yes) had a quick brow shaping.

No, it wasn't until I was walking down East Fifth Street at exactly 6:58 p.m. that I felt the unmistakable spasms of anxiety, which seemed to indicate that I might have once again set myself up for an encounter that could, if one were to look at it quite objectively, be tremendously awkward and disappointing.

I suddenly found myself gripped by the terrifying thought that I was so obviously made-up and coiffed, meticulously manicured and hypergroomed, that I may as well have worn a sign announcing my availability, measurements, and utter lack of shame or pride.

There was still time for damage control, I thought. I dug through my bag in a futile search for a tissue, but to no avail. I ducked into a deli and quickly bought a bottle of water and some Kleenex. I prided myself on noticing the super-hot man in line behind me. He was purchasing wintergreen Dentyne. See, I thought to myself, there were plenty of attractive, sexy men for me to ogle and woo. No need to rashly pin all of my hopes and desires on Colin Bates. Tess was right—I hadn't even *seen* him. He could be hideous, after all.

I chided myself. *So* like a *woman* I was, not even to consider the fact that *I* might not be attracted to *him*. I had ascribed all of these heroic qualities to a person that I had never even seen before! I had the power here, I told myself. At least I knew that Dentyne man was concerned for his breath, which was more than I knew about Colin Bates!

I was leaning over the ice-cream freezer, stealing snatches of my reflection in its metal door handle as I dutifully engaged in my make-under when I heard my cell phone ring.

"Hello."

"Hey, Lena. It's Colin."

"Hey," I said meekly. Just hearing his voice made me smooth out my hair and wish I hadn't smeared so much lipstick off. I was hopeless.

"Listen. I'm in a deli on Fifth Street. What was the address of the café again?" His voice was echoing as if he were standing right next to me.

He's in a deli on Fifth Street.

"Wait, *I'm* in a deli on Fifth Street," I said, with a bit more of a quaver than I would have liked. Instinctively, I turned my head toward the cash register. And there before my eyes, was Dentyne man, clutching his pack of gum…and a cell phone. And he was mouthing my name.

"Hi," Dentyne man's mouth and Colin's voice said to me simultaneously. Dentyne man broke out into a wide smile as I slowly walked toward him.

"Colin Bates." He shook my hand with a firm grasp.

"Lena Sharpe," I said, still dazed.

"What were you doing back there?" He looked puzzled.

"Uh." Rapid flashback to furious lipstick removal gave way only to the more horrifying realization that I was having my first introduction to Colin Bates under the cruel gaze of fluorescent deli lights which, very likely, were rendering my pores to be the size of Frisbees.

"I was, I felt a little warm, so I was just…wiping down with some…" *Wiping down?*

"Bottled water?" He was trying to help out.

"Yes," I said, as if this were supposed to make perfect sense.

"I hope you're not getting sick. Because we can do this another—"

"No. Oh, no. I'm just…the subway, you know. It can

be...warm. That's all." I smiled brightly, determined to sweep this entire subject under the rug. "So, how are you?"

"I'm good." He seemed either amused or perplexed, I couldn't tell which.

Yet, despite all of my insecurity and discomfort, I was still able to perform the necessary mental assessment of the newly revealed Colin Bates. He was, quite simply, my type. Now that is not to say that I in fact had a quantifiable type previous to this encounter. I could not, for instance, rattle off a series of distinctive qualities (sandy-brown hair, angular build, penchant for natural fibers, for instance) and conjure up a clear picture of my ideal man. It simply seemed to be one of those innumerable situations where you knew something when you saw it. And I was seeing it stand before me now in a neon-bright deli on East Fifth Street. His dark brown hair was perfectly tousled, with a lock or two grazing past his large brown eyes. He was tall but not too tall, muscular but not brawny, his clothes were well selected but not overly thought out. I looked down at his shoes, and then smiled to myself. Excellent STP.

"How was your trip down?"

"Oh, it was good. I made good time."

Silence. Deli lights. Gigantic pores.

"We should go," I said with sudden urgency, and started out the door. "It's just down the block."

Once outside in the cool and blessedly dark night, I calmed down somewhat. Of course, my brief infusion of self-empowerment had evaporated as I felt the intoxicating glee at having my unreal fantasies about Colin Bates become suddenly and stunningly real.

But now, the initial question reemerged, rearing its ugly and oh-so-familiar head. The three desperate words of the serial dater were upon me—Is...he...interested? But even more pressing at this point was this question: Is this a date?

"Listen, are you hungry?" He turned to me suddenly.

The correct answer seemed to be yes. Dinner = Restaurant + mood lighting + alcohol = Date?

"Oh, but you might not have a lot of time?" He started to answer his own question.

"Not at all." I practically cut him off. "Where did you have in mind?"

"I know this great place." He seemed excited. Excitement + premeditated destination = Date?

We walked a few blocks east until we reached the outer fringes of Alphabet City. On an abandoned stretch of Avenue D, he led me toward an unmarked storefront. Through the dusty panes, a warm light glowed and lively Latin music escaped as the door swung open and closed, exchanging patrons.

"What do you think?" he asked.

What I was thinking was: loud burrito joint + bustling college crowd ≠ Date. What I said was: "It looks perfect." I even managed a smile. It was still early, I thought.

And so we made our way to the back of the cantina, negotiating Corona-swilling revelers at every turn before finally securing a cozy banquette for two. Within seconds, a waiter and two margaritas had appeared.

"They know me here," he said, glancing at the drinks.

"I see." I smiled back at him.

"Thanks for indulging me. It's just so great to be back in the city. I wanted to celebrate a little," he said.

First night back in the city + plans with me + alone = Date?

"Please, it's my pleasure. It's one of the more exciting business meetings that I've had in a while." Could I have possibly sounded more dorky? And why had I mentioned business?

"Well, I'm glad to hear that." He leaned forward on the table, pushing his shirtsleeves up to expose his (quite masculine!) forearms.

He's "glad to hear that" + slow, forward lean = Date?

I took a sip of margarita. A long, long sip. I knew I shouldn't get drunk, but the instinct to give myself to the moment—and escape this vise of awkwardness—was strong. If only I knew what this *was.* I wish I could talk with Tess—she would know what this was. No, I took that back. She would tell me that I should hold back regardless of what this was and then she would grill me as to whether *I* really liked *him,* until I became convinced that not only was he not the one, but that the very concept of finding "the one" was flawed.

I looked over at Colin surreptitiously while he eyed his menu. He had to have flaws. Everyone has flaws, right? His head was down now. I could make out just the faintest pattern of…was that a patch of baldness? No, that was the light…but it might be thinning just a tad. Colin looked up suddenly. I was caught. I froze for a second. Our eyes locked. Then his face gave way to a warm, beautiful smile that made me feel as if I'd melted into a gelatinous, gooey mess in front of him. Okay, Tess, I thought to myself, he has no flaws, I'm sorry.

"So, do you know what you want?"

Could that be a double entendre?

"I'm having the enchilada, my standard," he offered. "You should try the shrimp with mole sauce. It's delicious, if you don't mind garlic."

Recommending garlic? Not a date.

"So, how did you find this place?"

"My ex-girlfriend used to live upstairs… Oh, I see Paco. I'll be right back."

I really don't know how much more explicit he could

be. Ex-girlfriend mention + escape from table for chat with his pal Paco = Not a Date. I could feel disappointment flood my body.

When he returned to the table, I was ready for business. At least he didn't have to know how silly and misguided my imagination had been. I could still save face. I ran through the breakdown of what he needed to do for the interview, explained the format, and gave him a list of proposed dates and locations for the taping. Colin listened patiently, asked pertinent questions and nodded encouragingly throughout my presentation. When I finished, I sat back in my chair, hands folded. He looked back at me, a sly smile creeping onto his face.

"Well, now I have some questions for you," he said.

I must have looked a bit startled as he leaned forward and touched my forearm (touched my forearm!) and said, "Don't worry, I'll keep it deeply personal." (Dare I even say it…hope crept back into my sad heart…rhymes with late!)

For the next ten minutes or so, he began to question me about my background, my family and my interests, as if he were, well, "interested." I was at a loss. I didn't know how I was supposed to behave, how candid I should be. In at least two instances, I even noticed that I had become fully engaged in the conversation, free of my usual omniscient observer voice. I lost track of time, of my "date self," and, alas, of the number of margaritas I had merrily imbibed.

And I felt okay with that. The room had melted into soft focus, my food tasted delicious, the music was divine, and I felt like I could sit there together with Colin forever. Maybe, I thought, it's okay not to know. I sighed audibly.

"What are you thinking about?"

My mind went blank. I felt sure that he must know what I was thinking about. Wasn't it all over my face? I'm in love with you! I'm thinking about our children's bone structure! I'm hoping that you're going bald so that women lose interest in you and you don't stray from me ever!

"What are *you* thinking?"

"Hey, I asked you first!"

"No, no, no. I'm the journalist," I teased.

"Oh, right," he smiled. "And I'm the subject."

"Exactly."

"And, as such, you are in the position of power."

"Absolutely." I smiled, liking the inference, despite the fact that I knew how far from reality that assessment was.

"I guess I *have* to tell you what I'm thinking, then."

"I'm afraid so."

"Okay, then, I was thinking—" he paused seductively "—about my mother."

I felt the cold shock of his answer slap me squarely in the face.

Colin chuckled (a deep, raw, easy laugh of course), realizing the impact of what he had said.

"Let me finish." He leaned forward. "I was thinking about how I should trust my mother's opinion more."

I shifted in my seat, trying on the new explanation, not sure whether it had helped.

"The interviewer needs more clarification."

"Hmm…the interviewee might become embarrassed."

"The interviewer insists."

He looked, I thought, for the first time, almost shy.

"I'm just kidding." I had to let him off the hook. "Let the viewer decide."

Colin didn't respond at first, just smiled with his eyes cast downward.

"My mother—" he paused "—said that you were a lovely young woman."

I felt a confident smile spread slowly across my face as under the table I squeezed the side of my chair for dear life. Date.

"Hello…Hellooo. I know you're there, Lena Elizabeth Sharpe. Lena. Lena? Now I'm worried. You're worrying me. I know you would automatically come to the phone for your dearest friend in the world, Jake Dunn, if you heard him calling…so I'll wait. Okay, now I'm getting impatient. How *will* I pass the time? Maybe I'll start by recounting your brief but oh-so-steamy fling with the coat-check boy at Lotus. Okay, you forced me. Mrs. Sharpe, Mr. Sharpe, if either of you are there, I apologize, but I do this all in the effort of teaching some phone manners to your daughter who has once again stood me up for our breakfast meeting. His name was Rico. Yes Rico—"

"Jake?" I answered finally. I had been in the middle of a deep sleep and couldn't tell if I had dreamed that the phone was ringing or if it really had.

"Ha! You are there."

"What time is it?"

"Noonish, I think."

"Wait, we weren't meeting until one, I thought."

"Oh, I know. I was just building the drama. And why are you screening *my* calls. Don't you know you're to be reachable for me at all times?"

"I guess I just lost track of my priorities there for a moment."

"Don't let it happen again." He was only half kidding. "Can you get down here, say, now?"

"Oh, Jake, I haven't even gotten out of bed yet."

"Wait, whoa, hey now. Explain yourself, young lady."

"I wouldn't know where to begin." I was smiling to myself now as I let the previous evening's surrealness wash over me, relieved that it wasn't a dream.

"Um, at the beginning. And in vivid, graphic detail, please."

"I need a second just to process it all myself."

"Okay, here's the deal. Multitask for me. Get in the shower, 'process,' and then get your lovely ass down to Kenmare and Delancey. Stat."

"Yes, sir."

"That's better."

I lay motionless in my bed, staring at the ceiling, replaying the better moments of the night before in vivid, graphic detail. It was almost as if I were able to be there again, only I could smooth over the anxiety-ridden parts and meld together the beautifully surprising ones.

He had walked me back to my apartment—to the door, not just to the corner like so many others who believed that that was far enough to be chivalrous and convenient enough to get a cab on the Avenue. I'm a "lovely young woman," I said to myself, smiling.

Of course, my bliss soon gave way to a mild panic as my mind raced down the list of morning-after questions. What next? How did we leave things? Did he know I was joking when I told that story about the thing? Did my breath smell? Oh God, what time was it? Oh Jake! I sprang out of bed and sprinted for the shower.

My hair was still dripping wet when I got out of the cab at Jake's pronounced destination.

"Oh, my lady, I didn't realize that we had advanced to cab transportation during the daytime hours."

"I was afraid to be late. You might have started calling up my ex-boyfriends."

"Mmm…good idea for next time."

"So, what's up with this mysterious location?"

He looked me up and down suspiciously. Clearly I would not be able to simply skirt the issue of my previous night's dalliance. "Okay, Sharpe, but don't think you're getting off the hook."

"I'm not trying to get off the hook," I smiled. I couldn't *stop* smiling.

He held my gaze for a second longer, cocked a glib, half smile and turned on his heel.

"Follow me." He proceeded forward to an abandoned storefront, quite casually kicked the door in, and called to me impatiently from the other side.

"Uh, Jake—this is eerily reminding me of the *Brady Bunch* episode when Bobby gets in trouble for going into the condemned building to save the cat."

"Um, while I applaud the Brady allusion, Lady Lena, I must implore you not to be such a Marcia."

"Okay, but if Mike and Carol come down here, I'm so blaming it all on you."

I stepped through the makeshift door to find a dusty, dilapidated interior. Jake stood in the middle, leaning against a rusty pipe with expectant eyes.

"What do you think?"

"I love it?" That seemed to be the only acceptable answer.

"Are you kidding me? It's horrible. But that's not the point." He waved away the space's present state as if it were just a minor annoyance.

"Okay, enough with the suspense. What really is the point here?"

"I've decided that this will be the site of my first art opening."

"Wait. What? Didn't we just talk on Thursday? When did

you become an aspiring artist?" Truth be told, Jake *was* a talented painter, but he was one of those people who was talented at so many things.

"Oh, you silly, silly girl. Don't you know me well enough at this point to understand that I'm much, much, much, much, much too smart to be an artist?" The very word dripped off his tongue with condescension. He was definitely worked up. "Hello? Sell my soul and sacrifice my lifestyle so that one day—if I'm frightfully lucky—my backbreaking work can hang over some pretentious fuck's living room sofa? I don't think so." Was he shuddering with disdain?

"So, enlighten me then," I said flatly.

"I am going to be—" he paused for dramatic effect "—an art *dealer*."

"So—" I paused, just to annoy him "—you're going to be the one selling the paintings to the pretentious fucks."

"Exactement!" And then he added quickly, "For an obscenely immoral commission." I thought he might burst with excitement.

"But, and I do mean this respectfully, what do you really know about art?"

Jake lowered his head, shaking it back and forth as if he were more disappointed in me than usual.

"Lena, Lena, Lena. I'll walk you through this gently." He clasped his hands together and began pacing. "In all the time that you've known me, I've been throwing parties, have I not?"

"You have."

"And tell me. Who are the people that always, always, always want to crash these parties, but are always woefully unsuccessful? Think Lena."

"Lame, uptown people?"

"Very good! Now, it's a rather simple equation that I actually fault myself for not arriving upon sooner."

"What's the equation, Jake?" If I didn't know him, I'd think he was crazy. Sometimes, I still had to wonder.

"Rich people want what I have, what I like. They want the lifestyle, the street cred, the beautiful women, the finger on the pulse of this city, if you will." He was frantic now. "And, of course, we both know that they will never, ever get that from me. But…but! I would be more than happy to provide them with the *illusion* of this dream. Sort of like a nice poster print of a famous work of art."

"So, it's really a charitable venture?"

"Perfectly captured, Ms. Sharpe!" And then he paused. "Oh, I can't even stand it—have you seen the things that these people buy? I don't know why I didn't think of it sooner." This point seemed to plague him. "And I can throw parties while I'm at it." His body relaxed, he was spent. "Don't you just love it when things make *sense?*"

"How are you going to get this place in shape?" I cringed with visions of myself splattered with paint and plaster.

"That part's even better! I can leave it practically as is— uptowners love thinking they've found something…*raw.*" His eyes gleamed.

"Oh, Jake. You're too much."

He took my hand and gave me a twirl, wrapping me up in his embrace. "Does that mean—" he lowered his voice seductively "—that I'm finally enough for you?"

"I'm the one who's not enough for you and we both know it."

"Tease!" He spun me out of his embrace with a laugh. "All right. Let's get out of here before the cops come."

"Jake! I *knew* we weren't supposed to be in here!"

"Oh relax, Lena, I'm going to get the lease. I just haven't done all the paperwork."

"Like write a paper check or pay with paper money."

"Something like that," he smiled. "Okay, I'm starving. Let's run over to Habana. I'll buy you a mojito to make it up to you."

We slid into our booth at Café Habana and ordered our usuals without a glance at the menu.

"And two mojitos please, señorita." Jake winked at the tan, taut waitress, who giggled a shy "de nada" and floated away.

"You're very sweet, but I don't know if I can look at another drink right now."

"Oh, yes." Jake's eyes lit up with the delightful anticipation of another "Lena losing it" story. "What was it—another martini marathon? Or was it a cosmopolitan collision? I warned you about the pink drinks, didn't I?"

"Margaritas," I said.

"Ah. So, you're in Tex-Mex detox today, huh? How many did it take?"

I thought for a second. "Three, I guess. I wasn't keeping track."

"Three?" Jake's voice reeked of disappointment. "You are *such* a girl."

"It wasn't just the alcohol."

"Oh, it wasn't *just* the alcohol." He had a way of making me feel like I'd said more than I should have. "Oooh, were we experimenting with the more adventurous opiates?" He couldn't have looked more pleased.

"No, I think it was the company."

"What? Let's see. I hope to God it wasn't Nick."

"It's not Nick."

"You met someone new? Did we not just talk on Thursday?"

"I sort of knew him already. You sort of know him, too."

"Hmm…okay, cut the mystery act, Miss Marple. Who?"

"Colin," I blurted out his name in an excited stage whisper.

"Colin Bates?" Jake raised his voice.

"Shhh!" I panicked.

"What? Why?" He seemed annoyed.

"Someone here could know him. *He* could be here for all I know."

"Oh, please, I'm sure Lord Colin hasn't stirred from his mansion yet."

"He's not like that, Jake."

"Is that so?"

"Jake, he's really great. Last night was…" I searched for the word that would properly convey the magical quality of the previous night without using the automatically gag inducing word *magical*.

"Magical," I sighed, knowing the reply already.

"Oh, God." Jake's face contorted in disgust.

"Jake, stop it. I'm serious."

"What happened to your whole ethical dilemma about dating someone from the show, anyway?"

In fact, the dilemma was still there, growing uncomfortably in the back of my mind. Before last night, it hadn't seemed necessary to address it, but now things were different. At least I hoped they were.

"I'll deal with that in my own time," I said unconvincingly.

"May I remind you that you don't even know him?"

"I'm *getting* to know him—"

"Well, when you get to know what a spoiled-ass jerk he is, let me know."

"Jake, I don't get it. Since when do you hate Colin? You don't even know him."

He ignored me. "Jesus, please tell me you're not going to go through this whole thing again."

"Go through what again?"

"This." He was getting agitated.

"What?" So was I.

"This whole thing where you make him into something he's not. Just don't put this one on a pedestal, okay?"

The waitress set down our drinks. I took a sip of mojito, it tasted sour and acidic, and felt the previous night's unexpected, unbelievable magic slowly wash away.

I stirred my cappuccino nervously. I had just given Tess an abbreviated version of the Colin experience. I didn't have the energy for the full-on dissection that I would usually give to such monumental encounters—or the resiliency to absorb a Tess reality check.

"Well, see where it goes," Tess said absently. Her mind was elsewhere, I realized, as I noticed her gaze predictably wander to the current coffee-maker on duty, referred to by us, his acolytes, as Macho Macchiato.

"What can I do to make you go talk to him?" I said, watching her watching him.

"I *have* talked to him," Tess replied. "He gave me change for a five last week."

We both stared at him intently.

"I think it's his eyes," Tess remarked with finality.

"Sure. And his rippling chest runs a close second."

"You're right. God, I'm as bad as a guy."

"Uh, no. If you were a guy, you would have already humiliated yourself with at least ten vain attempts to impress him."

"See! By your own admission, I would 'humiliate' myself if I were to approach him." She looked vaguely triumphant.

"You, Tess, would not humiliate yourself."

"No, I wouldn't, because I would never, ever deign to

frolic with someone who is, quite likely, an out-of-work actor just getting by ladling lattes." Tess had taken on her self-righteous, "my great-great-great-grandfather came over on the Mayflower" voice that she only assumed when she was unsure of herself. Which wasn't very often.

I didn't respond. We resumed our reverent observation. He *was* a fine specimen. Tess had discovered him more than six months ago and, ever since, we had bypassed three Starbucks, two New World Cafés, and a Saint Alp's tearoom so that we could sit here at French Roast and argue over whether or not Tess should ever break the fourth wall and approach Macchiato himself. Mostly, however, we just had idle conversation punctuated by long, dreamy staring sessions. I enjoyed seeing this side of Tess, but my mood today was somewhat confrontational.

"What's the pleasure in just watching him if you never intend to act on it?"

"It's a crush. It will pass." She stirred her chai latte in measured, steady turns like a testy cat swishing its tail. I decided to ignore the signs.

"Maybe it could be something more?"

She was silent for several seconds and then: "Lena, this guy's very likely jailbait. And it's even more likely that he's entirely vapid. Why ruin the view with reality?"

"You're so cynical," I said, slouching down in my chair.

"I'm realistic. You should try it sometime."

"What do you mean by that?"

Tess put down her mug. Her brow furrowed and I knew she felt badly.

"Lena, I'm sorry."

"I know you are." My voice softened.

"I just don't have that much faith in happy endings, I guess."

"Like with me and Colin?"

Tess didn't respond, thus answering my question.

"Jesus, what does everyone have against Colin? I'm not crazy. We *did* have a great time."

"What do you mean? Who else is giving you a hard time?" She seemed alarmed that someone else might have taken on the cynic's role in my life.

"Jake."

"Well." Tess gave a beleaguered half smile. "Jake may have a different agenda than I do."

"What do you mean?"

"Oh, never mind, you'll tell me I'm crazy and it's not worth it."

"Okay, now you *have* to tell me."

"Jake's jealous."

"You're crazy."

"What did I tell you?"

"But I've dated lots of guys since I've known Jake."

"Yeah, and hasn't he hated most of them?"

"Well, yeah."

"There you go."

"But you should have heard him, Tess. This was not like the others. He seemed so pissed off when I was telling him about our date."

"Well." Tess paused. "Maybe he senses something different about this one."

"Like what?"

"Like you like him more than the others."

"I do, Tess. I mean, I really think I do."

"Then, there's your answer." She patted my hand. "Jake's a sensitive guy, Lena. He *gets* you."

"Then he should be happy for me, not jealous because I want to spend time with someone else."

But Tess's attention was elsewhere right now. She glanced

at her empty coffee mug and then motioned to the front counter, her eyes dancing mischievously toward her Macho Macchiato.

I walked out of French Roast with a heavy heart. I was annoyed—how had my beautiful, magical (yes magical!) night become so tainted? Wasn't my own self-doubt enough to deal with? Now I had to wrestle with the doom and gloom of my supposed best friends?

My mind flashed to moments from the previous night, moments that made my heart leap. Yes, it *was* still real. I walked faster—abusing my Sigerson Morrisons as they pounded the pavement. I didn't see the people around me, but I was being propelled by their energy, the city's energy— powerful, positive energy that didn't question motive or agenda, energy that gave a girl a chance, for God's sake. Wasn't that what this city was built on? I was getting worked up.

At some point, I forgot where I was going with such de- termination. I guess I could walk home, but what would I do there? The deep void of Saturday night yawned before me. I couldn't call Tess; I wouldn't call Jake. And then the dreaded questions began to fill my head: Would he call? Had he called? And the one that I personally hated the most: Should I call?

Of course, the moment these questions enter one's mind, one knows that the honeymoon has indeed ended, the mag- ical post-great-date period as it were, has ceased. I reached for my cell phone. I had two choices—I could either check my messages now or wait until I got home.

There were downsides to both scenarios. If I were to check now and not hear anything, I would very likely lose the urgency to walk home. I would feel also as if I'd jinxed the process by calling my own phone (what if he couldn't get through because we happened to call at the exact same time? A remote possibility, but a possibility all the same). On the other hand, waiting until I arrived home presented the problem of placing an enormous amount of pressure on my arrival. I hesitate even to contemplate the idea of discovering the steady, unblinking red light of my answering machine—the cruelest mocking of a single woman ever known. The very thought made me tense. I punched in the numbers without thinking, without seeing. And I waited. It would be way too soon for a call even if he were completely in love with me, I thought, trying to prepare myself for disappointment. Would I even want someone that was so quick to violate dating etiquette? My powers of self-protective rationalization were at high alert. I heard my message (God, how I hated the sound of my own voice. That message alone would likely drive him away) and then the short tone followed by the cruel words "No New Messages."

"Hello?" I heard a disembodied voice speaking to me.

I held my phone to my ear. Had I hit speed dial by accident? Was I truly going crazy?

"Hello?" I answered.

"Lena? Is that you?"

"Yes." I put my ear to the phone. "Who is this?"

"Hey, it's Colin."

Hey, it's Colin? I was stunned. "Hi."

"That was so weird. I wasn't sure if my call went through. All I heard was rustling."

"I just hung up another call," I said. It was beginning to make sense. "You must have called just as I hung up."

"Wow, what are the chances of that?"

"Very remote," I said with a slow smile. Slim to none.

"So listen, I was just wondering what you're doing tonight?"

chapter 7

Each night, Colin took me somewhere new. I had lived in New York for five years and had done my share of exploring, but Colin knew the city far more intimately. We each played our part—discoverer and discoveree—with equal enthusiasm. The restaurants and cafés he knew weren't fancy or pretentious (or even mentioned in Zagat's). Most often, they were tucked away like private kitchens that just happened to have a table for two in the corner.

That night in particular, it happened to be a small Greek tavern in Queens.

"You're probably the only date I've had that's taken me to Queens for dinner," I said.

"You're probably the only date I've had who would appreciate it," he replied.

We stared at each other. He would do this often—hold my gaze until I would blush and look away. Then he would laugh. Then I would laugh. Bliss.

"So, how did you find this place?"

"Well, I had a tendency…" He paused. "I guess we know each other well enough at this point for me to tell you."

My heart leaped at the inference! And then stopped for a beat when I considered what he might tell me.

"Caleb and I used to have a habit of skipping school," he said finally.

"That's awful," I said with relief.

"I know, I know. Anyway, we would get on the train and just take it wherever—the Bronx, Harlem, all over. We got lost once in Astoria and Milos helped us out. He owns this place."

"He didn't report a couple of city boy truants?" I said playfully.

"Not until he fed us some oysters and scared us with a few navy stories."

How I loved his romantic boyhood mischief stories! I half expected him to tell me his real name was Huckleberry.

"Did your mom ever find out?"

"Mmm…yeah." His face soured.

"How?"

Wordlessly Colin rolled up his shirtsleeve. Just below his tricep, there was a faded blue tattoo—the kind you see on ex-cons or WWII vets. "Bonnie" it read.

"Who's Bonnie?" I said, confused.

"I don't remember. Caleb picked it out. I was too drunk. We were going to have our girlfriends' names tattooed on our arms like Milos, but the artist mixed them up." He looked embarrassed.

"What was the name supposed to be?" I asked.

Colin paused. Direct eye contact. "Lena."

"Yes?" I answered, my voice barely audible.

"No," he smiled, and said in a whisper, "That was the name." He leaned in closer to me.

"I don't think I believe you."

"Well, it's the only name I can possibly think of right now." With that, he leaned over and kissed me.

Of course, if I were a stranger listening to this exchange with Colin, I would very likely immediately vomit, but as a participant in the conversation, I had to admit that it all felt genuine and real, and completely divine.

"You know, Colin, there's something I should talk to you about as well," I said. I had been dreading this conversation, but I had to say something.

"What is it?"

"Well, it's just that the fact is I'm doing a story on you for the show."

"Right." Colin reached forward for my hand.

"And some people might be a little surprised to know that we've been hanging out—" I searched for the right words "—in a more personal way."

"A more personal way?" Colin smiled at the phrase.

"I'm not sure how to handle things, that's all," I said, not looking up.

"What were you thinking?" he asked.

I paused. "Well, we could hold off until your segment's done," I said, barely able to get the words out.

"Is that what you want to do?" he asked.

"This isn't about what I *want*," I said.

"Well, do you know what I think?" Colin said softly, running his fingers along my wrist.

"What?"

"I think that we should keep work at work—" he paused "—and we should keep our personal relationship—" he bent down and kissed my hand "—personal. Does that sound good?"

I must have known that there was a choice of answers to

this question, but in that moment, only one seemed possible. "Yes," I said, my voice barely above a whisper. God, I was so weak. I felt myself blush. I had very likely been blushing the whole time.

"I love the way you blush," he said with a smile.

"You do?" It was so strange the things that he would compliment—my squeaky hiccups, the way my hair always fell in my face. He liked the things that I tried to change, to smother out or at least ignore.

"Yeah, it shows that you're sincere."

"Oh, does it?" I tried to be coy—but sincere. Sincerely coy?

"Yeah." He leaned forward. "And it's really sexy."

"You certainly know how to embarrass me, don't you?" I raised my hands to my face, which he promptly pushed away, covering my cheek with his palm. He felt cool. I felt drunk.

Up until this point, my entire dating life seemed like one long audition process, an ongoing attempt to tweak my appearance and/or behavior in the effort to attract the right member of the opposite sex. With Colin it was different. Never before did I think that my tendency to turn red when put on the spot, to trail off sentences, to leave my clothes in little piles throughout my apartment could be seen as "endearing," "alluring," or even "sexy."

I was not Sienna Skye. I never would be. No makeup trickery or well-placed accessory would ever change that. A guy like Colin could certainly woo a Sienna Skye if he wanted to. Couldn't he? Wondering what caught his interest in me was both terrifying and exhilarating.

"What do you want to do?" Colin asked, lightening the mood a bit.

"Mmm…I'm fine right here."

"Come on, I only get a few hours with you a day. I want to maximize it."

He was right, it was only a brief time each night, but it felt somehow like a different day altogether, a separate life. At last, the tyrannical monotony of work-subway-dinner-TV-sleep was broken. With Colin, the most banal event became a grand opportunity for adventure and discovery. Have you ever eaten Ethiopian—yes, but not with you! Just walking along the tacky shops on lower Broadway had been transformed into something like a Moroccan bazaar—look at those magnets! Oh, and those two each with our names on them! Suddenly it didn't seem at all strange to be excited by the same street fair that rotated throughout the city every other weekend. Making dinner became fun, browsing books at Borders was a new world of discovery, standing in line at Duane Reade was a distinct pleasure.

"Hey, do you want to go to a party?" he asked excitedly.

Suddenly I heard the needle drag clumsily across the record of my beautiful fantasy. It was an indication of my state of mind, I suppose, that I found it plausible that I would never have to expand our world to include other people. Silly me.

"A party?" The idea of washing dishes with Colin was a joy, but the thought of interacting with his suave social set struck fear in my heart. My anxiety could be summarized in five words—I would not measure up.

"Yeah, it's just a few friends…it's no big deal." He sensed my hesitation. "Forget I said anything."

I calculated in my head the possibility of fooling Colin's entire cadre of friends into thinking that I was a suitable object of his affections. "No, we should go," I said. No, we shouldn't. No, we shouldn't. No, we shouldn't, I thought.

"Maybe you're right," he said.

No, I'm not. No, I'm not. No, I'm not! I'm wrong, so very, very wrong. We should never allow a third party into our world. Deal?

"We'll just stop by. How's that?" he said.

At that moment, my cell phone rang, providing a blessed delay. I reached down to get it and saw a text message from Jake: "I bought us tix for 9pm Casablanca at Screening Room. Meet me there? Peace."

It would be so easy. "I had plans," I could say. "I forgot all about them," I would explain. "You go on to the party, have fun," I would encourage him. I could spend the rest of the night with Jake. I wouldn't have to face Colin's world just yet; the fantasy could linger a bit longer. I could choose Jake or I could choose Colin.

"Let's go to the party," I said as I placed my phone back into my bag.

The party was not at all what I had expected. It was enjoyable.

One by one, I met the characters from Colin's stories as well as those who I had interviewed over the phone for the show. I knew their stories, but they didn't know mine, which felt like a distinct advantage. There were his "friends from a misspent youth," as he described it—the "misguided" (as Libby Bates had declared him) best friend, Caleb, and the cheerful, down-to-earth Cecily, who had an easy, melodic laugh. There was also Gavin, Colin's good-natured college roommate from Williams who was now a bespectacled lawyer, as well as Gavin's long-term girlfriend, Grace, a serious but sincere-seeming architect with a crisp British accent.

And then I saw Colin talking to…her. I had noticed the slim, shadowy figure twice before I realized that it was a person and not a glint of light. No such luck. She wore a simple silk dress that hung elegantly on her long, lean frame. She leaned against a column, staring dreamily at him as he talked while her fingers lingered lazily over the rim of a champagne glass. It was as if Daisy Buchanan, Veronica Lake and Gwyneth Paltrow had coalesced before my eyes. She was the source, I realized at that moment, of every woman's consuming neurosis, the obstinate itch that drove her to wax, pluck, dye, moisturize, exfoliate, and obsess over every flaw, perceived or otherwise. All of a sudden, I felt clunky and drab. Essentially, I felt like I did when I had my period, wore tapered leg pants, or ate at Taco Bell.

"She's too gorgeous, I know." Cecily was beside me now.

I winced at the words because they confirmed the worst—I wasn't hallucinating. She seemed too beautiful to be real, so maybe she wasn't real at all.

"Who is she?" I had meant to say the words casually. I had failed.

Cecily moved in conspiratorially.

"Malena," she said.

We shared a look, and in that moment, commiserated in the unspoken heartache and utter unfairness of our plight. This woman was a force of nature, a punishment sent by the gods, an ethereal specter named Malena—a woman who defied all principles of fairness, a woman who existed as living proof that you can in fact have everything, that models really are that beautiful—and skinny—in person, that it's not just the makeup and the hair and the lights. Damn her.

Mal Lena, I thought. Bad Lena. The symbolism was too much.

"But don't worry, she's dating a Venezuelan banker," Cecily offered.

I exhaled slightly.

"I think…"

I inhaled again.

"Or maybe they broke up." Cecily shrugged. "Either way, that was all years ago. High school."

What was years ago? I thought to myself. I could feel jealousy clinging to me like a cheap polyester dress. Any last drops of self-confidence quickly drained out of me, leaving me a dull, lifeless shell with flyaway hair and last year's shoes.

She looked at my expression, which must have spoken volumes. "Don't worry! Come on, let's go get another drink." Cecily, my new friend and ally, pulled at my arm, trying to save me from myself. But I wouldn't follow. I couldn't take my eyes off them. They stood together, still. She had taken a few steps back, I noticed, but then he had moved in to close the gap. Or had he? Cecily tugged my arm again and I reluctantly began my retreat to the bar—but not before I noticed Malena's long, fragile fingertips graze the side of Colin's arm. Or did they?

"What would you like?" Cecily asked me as we sat down at the bar. "Maybe a tequila shot to get rid of all that unpleasantness, huh?"

"You read my mind," I said, trying to manage a half smile. Cecily moved down the bar to get the bartender's attention.

"What unpleasantness?" I felt Colin's arm slip gently under my shirt. It was cool and seemed to salve the wound. Somewhat.

"You're back," I said.

"I missed you," he whispered in my ear.

"Your friends are pretty amazing," I whispered back, leaning into him, wishing away the previous apparition.

"You're sweet," he said, "but I bet they look pretty humble next to all your high-powered media friends."

"Colin, that's not true!" I chastised him. Did he really think I had high-powered friends? How funny that we were both intimidated by each other's worlds!

"I really like Cecily. She's great," I said.

"Yeah, Cecily's always been special," he said, focusing on her at the end of the bar.

"Hey kids, ready for a change in venue?" Caleb had appeared and threw an arm around each of us, ready to go. I'd met him in person no more than forty-five minute ago, but his familiarity now seemed perfectly natural.

"Oh, man. You're drunk already?" Colin teased.

"I'm not drunk at all, Mr. Bates. I'm merely relaxed and delighted to be in the company of friends. I'm high on life, if you will."

"Right. Does life usually present itself to you in the form of a martini glass?"

"He's quite the clever writer, isn't he, Lena?" He looked at me with a wink and then glanced back at Colin. "You've got yourself quite a woman there, Mr. Bates."

"Yes, I do. Yes, I do." And then I felt his arms circle around me, followed by a sweet kiss on the cheek. It was almost as if I'd never seen the golden apparition. Almost.

And just like that, I was officially part of the group—Caleb, Gavin, Grace, Cecily and one or two other alternates. Gavin would call me when he couldn't reach Colin. Caleb called when he saw something particularly inane on television (he joked that I was responsible for everything he saw on TV since I was the only one he knew who worked in the industry). He and I would laugh about that day's idiotic Jerry Springer display, I would gently chide him for his lack of a job, and then we'd make our inevitable plans to meet up that night. It felt so natural, so easy, so right.

It was as if I'd inherited a whole network of lifelong friends—complete with quirky, absurd nicknames, inside jokes and comfortable drunken repartee. All this and luscious Colin to boot? It was too much. Sometimes I worried that it was too good to be true.

And, in fact, it was. That much would be made clear to me just a few days later when I stepped into Vanessa Vilroy's apartment for the first time.

I had arrived alone—my first mistake. The apartment was the most beautiful loft I had ever seen. It was not merely loftlike as so many in the city purported their glorified studios to be. It was a gigantic, hardwood floor, stainless-steel kitchen, private elevator, exposed brick, postmodern *Architectural Digest* specimen. It was what money and style could create if someone was blessed enough to have both.

The elevator had deposited me right inside the living room, where I stood alone, drinking in the fabulousness of it all. I found myself walking forward, startled by the reverberating tap of my heels. My shoes suddenly sounded cheap and tinny in this apartment.

A young woman appeared, her face stoic.

"Hi," I said brightly.

"Hello," she said, waiting a beat.

She seemed neither fearful that someone was standing in her monstrous living space nor as if she were expecting guests. She just seemed slightly annoyed.

"I'm a friend of Colin's. I—"

"Is he on his way up?"

"Well, no. I mean, he will be. He didn't… We didn't come together…." I felt like an intruder. I felt like I was lying.

"You *are* Vanessa, aren't you?" I'd started to worry that I was in the wrong place, since I seemed to be the only guest at this party.

"Yes," she said. And then she turned, looking over her shoulder. "Would you like a drink?"

"Oh yes, please," I said, a bit too quickly, I thought. I watched her walk away. She was wearing faded Levi's that fit perfectly and a man's dress shirt. She was beautiful, of course, tall and slender, with glowing olive skin and straight black shiny hair.

"Here you go," she said, handing me a glass of white wine.

"Thanks." I smiled.

We stood there. I felt awkward. She seemed relaxed.

"That's a beautiful canvas." I looked over at a just-begun painting propped up against the wall.

"I just started it this morning."

A connection? Worth a shot, I began walking over to the painting.

"Would you mind?" Vanessa stopped me short. "Your shoes?"

"Oh, of course." I froze, thinking she was insulting my cheap, tinny footwear, then I looked down and saw her bare (perfect) feet. I slowly, carefully, removed my heels as if I were being instructed by a hijacker. I stood there in my un-pedicured feet, realizing that she had just stripped me of my one advantage—height. She now towered over me like an older, prettier, teenage sister. I was the awkward adolescent.

"Thanks." She looked satisfied.

I'd known Vanessa before. She was the kind of girl men lusted for, were intimidated by, and often left their girl-friends for—only to be tossed aside when she became bored (and she always got bored). She was the kind of girl who could look over a woman with one blisteringly critical sweep of the eye and leave her wondering for days what was so obviously amiss.

I hated her. And so of course Colin loved her. Several ex-cruciating moments later, when he finally walked through the door, the two embraced warmly and Vanessa's icy veneer seemed to melt down around them as they laughed and kissed, making some inscrutable shorthand joke that I was sure wouldn't make sense to me had I implored them to break it down for me word by word.

"Hey, Lena." Colin pecked me on the cheek lightly as if drained by his grand display of passion with Vanessa.

"Hey," I said, but he had already headed out to the kitchen. Obviously he knew his way around.

Another awkward silence followed as Vanessa and I stood together, alone once more.

"Those are such great paintings—" I would try again.

"Hey, Vanessa," Colin cut me off as he came out of the kitchen.

"Yes?" She smiled. She *smiled?*

"These paintings are fucking awesome. When are you having another show?"

Of course. *She* was the painter. The artist. The visionary. I knew it—she was "the art school girl," the bohemian rich girl who never wore makeup, never had a zit, had affairs with hot European professors, wore tank tops braless and managed to look sultry rather than slutty. I felt sure she took avant-garde photographs of herself nude.

Moments later, the door opened and the rest of the party spilled inside in one jovial pile. There was Caleb, Gavin, Grace and Cecily, of course—but also a couple of sullen, lank-haired boys clutching portfolio bags as well as one of the better-looking men I've ever seen. He wore a loosened tie and a cashmere coat and also happened to be a tenant of the gorgeous loft—Vanessa's significant other and, by all accounts, her home's primary funder.

And he was friendly. "Hey there, I'm Christopher," he said, shaking my hand warmly. How could he be so nice? He and Vanessa together, I thought, were like sweet and sour.

And so the night continued. Gradually I sifted through the various relationships, delineating who knew whom from Andover or summers at the Cape, or freshman dorms at Yale. One thing was clear—they had all met before. And, it seemed, the disparate lot had engaged in an unprecedented amount of collective revelry over the years. Stories were ignited by the mention of a seemingly innocuous phrase or word—asparagus! for example—which would then prompt an explosion of giggles and a string of nonsensical recollections—"And you ate the whole thing!" "He asked what time it was!" "She wore the purple sweater!" Colin had gradually slid off the ottoman next to me to assume his current position on the floor where he sat Indian-style as Vanessa playfully rubbed his feet.

"Hey, are you okay?" Cecily had sat down next to me.

"Oh, I'm fine," I lied.

"Look, Vanessa can be a lot to take at first." She looked at me meaningfully. "But she'll mellow out. She always does."

"God, I hope so." I felt some of my pent-up tension release.

"Look, we're a tight group. It can be hard to find your way in with everyone."

"Thanks, I'm so glad you said something. Really." How could one of Colin's female friends be so wonderful and warm and the other so cruel and cold? Even more strangely, I could tell from their interaction that Vanessa and Cecily were pretty close.

"Let's play a game!" one of the pair of sullen, lank-haired boys exclaimed, clearly unwound by his fourth glass of wine. His boyfriend was the only other "outsider" present aside from myself, but we had yet to even make eye contact, let alone speak to each other. It was as if he sensed Vanessa's contempt for me and shunned me to save himself.

A game? My stomach sank. Games required winners and

losers— picking teams, tests of knowledge, revelations of ig-
norance…this couldn't be good.

"I know—Truth or Dare!" Vanessa exclaimed.

The memories of countless adolescent slumber parties,
complete with wood-paneled rec rooms, HBO late-night
soft porn, and the unsanctioned use of shaving cream filled
my head. At the same time, the suggestion was completely
natural—Vanessa was the grown-up, urban version of the
same twelve-year-old girl with advanced breast development
and powers of exclusion that haunted every preadolescent
girl's life.

Before anyone could object, she quickly devised a list of
"rules," which she delivered with a jolt of authority that
seemed to make everyone forget she had just invented them.

"Okay, so I've put everyone's name in a hat. Colin, you'll
draw first and then we'll go around the room clockwise,"
she instructed.

I felt Colin lean back toward me, his hand resting on my
foot. I leaned forward, lightly massaging his shoulder—until
I realized that he was just reaching for the hat to draw a name.

Vanessa was perched on a velvet ottoman, her legs tucked
beneath her. All eyes were on her—a situation in which she
seemed extremely comfortable.

"Caleb, you're first," Colin said. "Truth or dare?"

"Dare," the room said in unison.

"Oh, I'm that predictable, am I?" And then he grinned.
"Dare."

Eruption of hilarity.

For the next ten minutes or so, Caleb entertained the
crowd by drinking five shots of tequila in a row, followed
by five raw chili peppers. The dare had only required three.

"Oh, Caleb, Jesus!" Colin was clapping his hands, nearly
as drunk—I imagine—as Caleb.

"You're next, man!" Caleb sputtered back.

Unfortunately, he wasn't.

"Lena?" Vanessa purred my name with faux sweetness. "Truth or dare?"

My mind was swimming. I generally always picked "dare" in these situations. After all, what's a little physical embarrassment among friends? Certainly it was preferable to the soul-bearing torture that a public Q&A session could bring about.

"What's it going to be?" Caleb yelled out. The crowd was restless, hungry for a sacrifice. How had I ended up here, I wondered, tipsy and traumatized in Vanessa Vilroy's Tribeca loft?

"Truth." I heard the word, but I was fairly sure that I had not uttered it. "Right, Lena?" Vanessa said. "You're a truthful person after all."

I didn't respond. I just sat there, dumbfounded. Who *was* she?

"Okay, truth," I said, looking Vanessa directly in the eye.

She returned the look with a slow, foreboding half smile, "That's what I thought." She didn't have to hesitate to think of a question. "If you found out that the love of your life still carried a torch for an ex-girlfriend, what would you do?"

I felt Colin shift beside me. Or did I? What was going on here? I was getting angry now.

"Hypothetically?" I said.

"Of course," she smiled.

"I need more details." I wanted to shift the spotlight— that was my strategy. It was not a good one.

"Well." She curled her arms around her feline body. "Suppose you find out that your 'hypothetical' boyfriend is still pining for his first love, though he would never ever tell you. He's a great guy, after all."

"Well, Vanessa, he can't be that great a guy if he's not being honest," Christopher spoke up. I love you, Christopher!

"He's a *fabulous* guy, dear," Vanessa shot back, "but you know how men can be."

"I'm not sure what you're asking me, Vanessa."

"Just answer the question, dear." She smiled at me sweetly.

The room had melted out of focus around us. It was just the two of us, my new nemesis and I.

"Your question, I'm afraid, has a faulty premise."

Vanessa straightened her back. She seemed thrown. I felt empowered.

"You see, the love of my life," I said, and paused for effect. My eyes locked with hers. "Would never stray."

I took a sip of wine and coolly sat back in my chair.

"He shifted."

"Stop it," Tess cautioned.

"His ass was probably just falling asleep," Parker offered. Tess shot Parker a look.

"Don't you think you might have been reading into the lean a little bit?" Tess asked.

"It was a shift," I corrected her. "Right when Vanessa asked me the question about 'the love of my life carrying a torch for someone else.' It really felt like she was trying to tell me something."

"Look, Lena, you're in the middle of the dance right now. Don't anticipate his every move. Just follow the music," Tess instructed me.

The dance. That was Tess's word for the period of time when an infatuation, a tryst, any sort of *connection,* could sink or swim. It was that period of hesitant phone calls and nervous dates; frenzied sex followed by awkward conversation—all of those initial experiences that mix together in a confused stew, tossed at random, ultimately either falling inward like a soufflé or very, very rarely, miraculously, coalescing into a fragile gossamer connection, known more commonly as "a relationship."

"But we never danced." I looked at Tess askance. "We clicked right from the start." I searched her eyes. "We *bypassed* the dance."

She looked at me, brows furrowed, concern creasing her face. But why was she concerned? I was *done* with that phase. I was *in* a relationship—the type of relationship I had always wanted. And yet, here I was, back at the table with Tess and Parker, psychoanalyzing Colin's changes in posture.

"Lena, you can't avoid the dance—as much as I know you would like to." Tess put her hand on mine. "It's like watching a movie—eventually the lights have to come on."

"Oh Jesus, what are you guys talking about?" Parker reached past me for the sugar tray.

"We're talking about Lena and her problem with Colin."

"Well," Parker said flatly, emptying a steady stream of Equal packets into her coffee. "I'm not convinced that Lena has a problem with Colin."

"Really?" I said, doubtful that Parker had even absorbed much of the conversation between her frantic cell phone calls and PalmPilot inputting.

She raised her head abruptly. "Lena, you met a friend of Colin's who you feel didn't mesh with you. Big deal. Don't start analyzing it to death or it *will* be about Colin."

"But, Parker—" I had to interrupt.

"Don't but me…" She looked serious. I shut up. "You will mess this up if you keep living in your head this way."

"Living in my head?"

"Look, I love you dearly—you know that. But you've got to realize that life doesn't always read like a Jane Austen novel."

With that, she gulped her sweetened coffee and rose to her feet, smoothing her Celine skirt. She smiled down at the two of us. "I've got to run to yoga. Some annoying hippie chick has been stealing my spot when I'm not there early enough. So *fucking* annoying!" And she was off.

"Yoga really has mellowed her out, hasn't it?" Tess joked, but I didn't respond. "Hey, Lena, don't let this Vanessa girl get you down. Just take it as it comes. It actually sounds like things are going pretty well with you and Colin."

"You think so?"

"Yeah, I do."

"Maybe I did overreact." I thought for a moment.

"Maybe a little, I think," she said.

"It's just so hard. His whole world can be a little intimidating."

"Lena, I know that world. I grew up in it. There's nothing to be afraid of."

"I guess. I can't believe you haven't even met him yet," I said.

"Yeah, I know. Has Jake met him?" Tess asked.

"Oh my God, Jake!" I caught my breath.

"What's wrong?" Tess said, alarmed.

"Oh, Tess, I just remembered. He asked me to go to the movies with him like a week ago and I totally forgot to call him back," I said, reaching for my phone. "I'll be right back." I hurriedly got up from the table to make the call. I tried all of his numbers, but all I got was voice mail. I left several long, apologetic messages and made my way back to Tess.

"Don't worry, Lena. He'll understand," Tess offered.

"Things have been weird. I've been preoccupied," I said, trying to remember the longest period of time that had passed during which Jake and I had not spoken since the day we met. This was it.

"Look, friendships like yours and Jake's are stronger than a forgotten phone call," Tess said gently.

"Of course you're right," I said. "Jake and I have something special." And I believed that. But still, I couldn't shake the feeling that something had shifted between us. And for the first time since I'd known him, I wondered when I would see Jake again.

chapter 8

"Let's go to the polo match this weekend!" Colin exclaimed a few evenings later as we finished a meal of take-out Thai.

I had been enthusiastic, of course, thinking it just an idle comment that would never come to pass—sort of like when someone says, "We should really go to museums more" or "Maybe I'll take a photography class." In a matter of moments, however, the plan was set. We would spend the weekend at Colin's parents' house in Easthampton, meet up with friends at Bridgehampton for the match, and then have everyone over for drinks that night.

That Saturday, I slowly made my way through a sea of linen and seersucker, trying to appear that I had seen a mallet used for something other than pounding meat a thousand times before. But where *was* I? What strange fashion meridian had I unknowingly crossed that suddenly sanctioned wide-brim hats and white shoes?

I was definitely in the Hamptons.

Easthampton, Westhampton, Southampton, Bridgehampton—they were like little clusters of Manhattan sprin-
kled along the eastern tip of Long Island, each with their
own personality and reputation. Socialites in Lily Pulitzer,
captains of industry in JP Tods, stately New England style
mansions with ferocious, hulking hedges connected like
Legos around their perimeters. People didn't go to the
Hamptons to "get away," they went there to stay inside, inside the frenzied bubble of social and professional kinesis
that occupied Manhattan for the rest of the year. From
Memorial Day to Labor Day, that energy briefly shifted
eastward by one hundred miles. Nick and Tony's replaced
Elaine's and Michael's. Lobster cookouts replaced champagne receptions. Marimekko replaced mink. But very little else changed at all.

Colin's house was beautiful, of course—just off Lily Pond
Lane, a stone's throw from the Perelmans and just south of
the Grubmans. His parents wouldn't be there (to my relief),
as they preferred their other home in the Vineyard. Why
two summer homes so close together? I had wondered, but
knew enough by now not to ask.

That morning, I had walked through the house exploring. I touched the furniture and felt the coolness of the marble on my bare feet. In the bathroom, I unpacked, using the
shelves and drawers even though we would be here just for
the weekend. I walked outside to one of the balconies. I
looked out at the ocean and inhaled the thick, salty air. You
never fully realized the toll the city took on you until you
managed to escape it.

Later on, as we roamed the Bridgehampton polo grounds,
however, the pressure had set in again with a vengeance.
Colin, of course, seemed to know everyone there, which
only made me feel more uncomfortable as I waited awk-

wardly for him to introduce me and then suffered the inevitable head to toe evaluation. For the moment, however, we were congregating with Colin's familiar crowd of Gavin, Grace and Vanessa while Caleb (of course) went to fetch us another round of drinks.

"Did you see Cecily with that guy?" Gavin asked, with a hint of mischief.

"No," I said, scanning the crowd. Good for Cecily, I thought.

"I did!" Grace chimed in. "They were hanging out in the owner's tent earlier. He was so hot!" she added, rather uncharacteristically.

"Hey, watch it there." Gavin pushed her teasingly.

"Well, he was." She smiled back at him.

"Oh, would you all calm down." Vanessa was grumpy. It was strange seeing her in the daylight. I thought she might evaporate in the sun.

"No way," Colin said. "She's not dating anyone. She's probably just flirting with one of the polo boys."

"Speak of the devil, here she comes." Gavin spotted her coming our way.

"Act normally. Like I didn't say a word," he instructed in an exaggerated stage whisper.

"Hey guys!" Cecily's eyes gleamed.

"Well, hello there." Gavin smiled knowingly.

So much for acting normally.

"What's new with you?" Grace asked expectantly.

"Oh, not too much," she teased us.

We all stood there awkwardly.

"Oh forget it, let's just cut to the chase. Grace and I saw you with that guy." I guess Gavin wasn't much for secrets.

"The *hot* guy," Grace corrected him.

"You brought a date?" Colin asked.

"Don't sound so surprised," she said, holding his gaze a moment. And then she smiled. "He *is* hot, isn't he? Actually, he just went to get another round of drinks. He should be on his way back now."

We all immediately swiveled our heads in unison to follow Cecily's gaze. And before my eyes, walking toward me at a leisurely gait, wearing an ivory linen suit and a bemused smirk was none other than Jake. My Jake.

"Hello there," he greeted us confidently, extending his hand for a round of firm, authoritative shakes.

"Jake?" My voice trembled. Maybe I was imagining things.

"Lena! What a surprise to see you here!" Jake said, looking not very surprised at all.

"You guys know each other?" Colin was confused.

"Yes," Jake answered for me. "I'm surprised she hasn't mentioned me. Lena and I go *way* back." He looked so pleased with himself.

"Isn't it a small world?" Cecily interjected happily. "Jake and I met in line at the Film Forum just last week. He was going to see *Breathless*—"

"Godard is a genius," Jake interjected.

"And I was going to see *Wings of Heaven*," Cecily continued.

"Because she's an angel," Jake cooed, slipping his arm around her waist and giving her a quick squeeze.

"But we started talking and it turned out we knew several people in common." Cecily smiled at me and then at Colin.

"That's right," Jake added. "When I realized that Cecily was a friend of Colin's, I was *shocked*."

I felt completely numb. I hadn't said a word yet and I wondered if I would ever be able to speak again.

"It must be fate then," Colin said dryly. He seemed annoyed or suspicious, I couldn't tell which.

"Do you come to the matches often, Jake?" Grace inquired, obviously still smitten. Wait, *Jake* was the hot guy everyone was so worked up about? It had just dawned on me.

"Used to, used to. Played a bit myself over the years." I shot him a look. He didn't waiver. "But you know, couple of broken ribs later, I told Peter I'd better just concentrate on my galleries."

Was he using a British accent?

"You know Peter Braman?" Gavin asked, clearly impressed.

"Oh sure, old friend, old friend."

Oh, for God's sake. Peter Braman was the publishing mogul and former top amateur player who had almost single-handedly brought the sport to the Hamptons. Clearly, both Jake and I had read his recent profile in *Vanity Fair*.

"You work in a gallery, I believe you said?" Grace inquired, still enchanted.

"He *owns* art galleries." Cecily was only too happy to make the important distinction. "He has another one opening downtown very soon."

I thought of the condemned space on the Lower East Side that he had brought me to that Saturday afternoon.

"I needed a New York presence," Jake offered ever so helpfully.

"He already has places in London, Milan, Saint Tropez, and…"

"Patagonia," Jake finished for her, and winked subtly at me.

"Must be tough times for you down there, what with the financial crisis, huh?" Colin said. Surely, he must know that he was talking to a complete fake. Jake was lying so wildly he might as well have declared himself royalty and worn a crown. This could not end well.

"Well, looks like the chukker's almost over," Jake announced abruptly.

Had he read *Polo for Dummies* on the jitney out here, I wondered?

"What do you say we head back over to the owner's tent, Cecily?" Jake said, ever so gallantly.

Thank God, I thought. And with a quick exchange of "pleased to meet you" and a knowing glance at me, Jake led his new lady away.

"We'll see you guys in a few hours, okay?" Cecily called over her shoulder.

Omigod. The cocktail party. I had completely forgotten. My first time hosting a party with Colin and my former best friend turned international gigolo would be attending.

"Well, Cecily certainly did well for herself," Grace concluded after the happy couple had escaped earshot. "I just can't put my finger on what it *is* about him."

"He certainly dresses well," Gavin offered.

"True," Grace agreed. "And he must be loaded."

"He's smoldering," Vanessa declared.

Even Vanessa was smitten?

"And you guys are good friends, huh?" Colin still looked uneasy. His nervousness, I was ashamed to admit, made me feel more secure than ever before.

"Yeah," I said, watching Jake go. We used to be, I thought.

"You're okay with Jake and me, right, Lena?" The party had just gotten started when Cecily wandered into the kitchen where I was busy slicing limes for a round of gin and tonics. I had spent most of my time up until this point avoiding Jake while also formulating the verbal attack I would unleash upon him when we were alone, back in the city.

My face tightened at the sound of his name. I closed the oven door gently, regained my composure and turned to face Cecily. She had taken a seat on the kitchen counter.

"Of course," I lied, and headed toward the refrigerator in an effort to avoid eye contact.

"I'm surprised he didn't tell you. I mean, I assumed he had. You two are pretty close, aren't you?"

I would have assumed the same thing, Cecily, I thought to myself, and started arranging biscotti on a tray.

"We really hit it off that night. We just have fun together." She smiled brightly. "I don't think I've ever met anyone quite like him." And then she laughed to herself, as if she'd just remembered something hilarious he'd told her. "And he's *so* funny!"

This was painful.

"But I have to ask." Her tone was more serious now. I experienced a brief moment of panic as possible questions that Cecily might "have to ask" about Jake filled my head.

"Why haven't you two dated?"

Well, that was an easy one. I was relieved.

"We're just friends. It would never work."

"Why not?"

"It's just not how our relationship is. We're such different people." There. That should placate her.

"What do you mean?"

Guess not. Jesus, these questions had to stop. She must feel insecure about Jake, I reasoned. It's only natural to wonder why a guy like Jake would be available. Sort of like when you find the perfect dress in a pile full of crappy ones on the last day of the sale. Something had to be wrong with it. Naturally she was turning him inside out looking for stains. My heart sank with sympathy for her. I chastised Jake in my head.

"What kind of girls does he usually go for?"

I pictured a montage of Jake's dalliances over the years and they coalesced into one indistinguishable perky blond prototype. I was pretty sure I couldn't tell her that Jake's relationships didn't last long enough to make such detailed assessments.

"Well…" I stalled.

"Am I making you uncomfortable? I'm sorry."

"No, not at all," I said, perhaps a little too vigorously.

"Listen, Lena. I just want—" She stopped herself midsentence.

"What?" Was she on to Jake? Was she on to *me?*

"I guess I just want something close to what you and Colin have." She shrugged. "If that's even possible."

I looked at her, speechless. My heart ached for her. She had been the first person in Colin's group to reach out to me and here I was deceiving her about Jake's intentions. Of course I knew he was going to have his fun with her, play his little games and move on to the next fling. And I felt complicit in his deceit—my hands were dirty, too.

"Cecily, darling," Jake was calling from the other room. "Come back in here, I miss you."

Cecily smiled. "Guess I better go." She slid off the counter to her feet. "Thanks for being so reassuring, Lena. We girls have to stick together, right." She gave me a quick hug and made haste to the arms of her Jake.

"And Lena." It was Jake again. "Could you be a doll and come freshen my drink when you have a moment? Thanks, love."

A few hours later, less familiar friends and acquaintances had headed out, leaving just the usual group of Caleb, Gavin, Grace, Vanessa, Christopher, Cecily, and of course, Jake—all of whom were splayed out lethargically throughout the room, each enjoying varying degrees of fatigue and drunkenness. The conversation had turned into an intense debate between Gavin and Christopher over the tax benefits of art collecting.

"That shouldn't be why you collect art," Gavin said idealistically.

"I'm just saying that sometimes there's an added incentive," Christopher added, practically.

"Art should be pure," Vanessa announced authoritatively, and took a long drag off of her Dunhill.

Oh get over yourself, I thought to myself as I cleared empty glasses away from the coffee table.

"Lena!" Vanessa erupted suddenly.

Oh my God, I panicked, had I said that out loud? I looked over at Vanessa, who now had her head slung back on the couch, her elegant fingers massaging her elegant temples. Maybe I had violently struck her in a blind rage?

"Would you *please* stop circling the room like that… you're making me nauseous," she said.

I paused, unsure of my next move. I didn't exactly want to take orders from Vanessa.

"She's a regular Cinderella, Colin," Vanessa said with a laugh.

"You're my little Cinderella, right, Lena?" Colin laughed. He was a little tipsy by this point.

"Are you that condescending to everyone, Colin, or just the women you date?" Jake said, shooting him a look.

The room was immediately silent.

"Ah, Jake." Colin broke the deadlock. "Lena didn't warn me about your sense of humor."

"Did she warn you about my volatile temper?" Jake asked, holding his gaze.

For a moment, the air felt thick with dueling testosterone. It seemed as if a fistfight might be the only way to break the tension. And then Jake's threatening scowl broke into a slow smile. "Just messing with you, man," he said. And Colin, at first confused, finally smiled, incredulously. He seemed embarrassed.

Slowly the room simmered back to its previous chatter level, but the party, for me, was long since over. I could see Jake eyeing me nervously. I knew he wanted to talk, but I didn't want to be anywhere near him. I whispered to Colin that I was going to bed, and I slipped up the backstairs through the kitchen.

Upstairs, I stood in the bathroom trying to make sense of what had just happened. Why was Jake here? I considered the idea that I might never speak to him again. I stared at my reflection under the fluorescent lights for a moment. I noticed a new tiny line extending out from the corner of my eye. A laugh line, I thought. What cruel irony. I wanted to cry, but I couldn't even summon tears.

I shut off the light and quickly got into bed. The sheets were tight and heavy, like a hotel. Everything in Colin's life felt like a hotel. After a while, I heard the door creak and then a gentle knock. Why would Colin knock?

"Lena?"

"Jake?" I bolted upright and turned to see Jake's silhouette coming toward me. Like in a horror movie.

"What are you doing? Get out of here!" A flash of terror shot through me as I imagined what would happen if anyone downstairs were to walk in and see Jake and me here in the dark, alone.

"Get out of here!" I was hysterical.

"Relax. They all went down to the beach for a walk," Jake said, taking a seat on the edge of the bed.

I calmed down a little—a little—as I remembered hearing the back door clatter shut.

"Everyone?" I asked suspiciously.

"Everyone, except Caleb. He's passed out drunk."

That sounded plausible.

"Jake, I really don't have anything to say to you right now," I said bitterly, but of course, I had *so* much to say to him. "What *was* that earlier? What are you even doing here?"

"The question should be, *What are you doing here, Lena?*"

"I'm dating Colin. Remember? He's my boyfriend."

"He's an idiot."

"Jake, of all the things you've done over the years—"

"Lena, did you hear the way he was talking to you? She's my Cinderella?" He looked like he wanted to spit.

"He didn't mean it like that, Jake. I think I know him pretty well at this point."

"God, can't you see it when someone's using you?"

"Do I need to remind you that you're in his house right now, Jake. You're a guest."

"I could give a shit about his house. Lena, you are *better* than this."

"And what are *you* doing here? Don't get self-righteous with me. You're just using Cecily to be here in the first place. It's horrible, Jake. She really likes you."

"Suddenly Cecily's your best friend?"

"She's a friend, yes. That's more than I can say for you right now."

"Oh, Lena, Cecily is just fine. I understand girls like her."

"Girls like her? Jesus, Jake, you're awful. You can't just treat people like they're disposable."

"Lena." He was serious now. "I know what Colin's about. And he sees your relationship as disposable. I know he does."

"You can't stand to see me happy, can you?" I was crying now.

"That's not it." Jake shook his head.

"Then explain it to me, Jake." I was exasperated. "Do you

realize *where* we're having this conversation? In Easthampton. In Colin's house. In his parents' bedroom, for Christ's sake. We're having this discussion in my boyfriend's parents' bed. This should not be happening." I looked at him, dumbfounded.

He bent his head down. His voice was quieter now. "You're in love with him, aren't you?"

"What?" I was confused.

"Just tell me, Lena," he said firmly.

"Yes, I am. I really am," I said. It was the first time I had acknowledged my feelings for Colin out loud and I felt dizzy. "Why would you ask me that?" I said, after a moment.

He didn't answer. "It doesn't matter," he said finally.

Suddenly I heard voices outside and splashes from the pool. Colin and the rest must have come back from the beach.

"I think they're back. You've got to get out of here," I said, feeling my panic return.

"Yeah," he said, getting up from the bed. "It's definitely time for me to go." And then Jake slowly walked away.

"Why are you whispering?"

"Colin's still asleep. I'm in the bathroom." I had just finished giving Tess a wrap-up of the previous night's drama. I was too distraught to wait until I got back to the city.

"Oh, you poor thing." Tess had taken on her maternal tone, which made me feel safe to cry.

"I just don't understand what happened. He came out here with Cecily, he picked a fight with Colin. It was crazy. Why would he do this to me?" I said, trying to sort through the weekend's events in my head.

"Honey, I know, I know."

"I mean, it was like he was trying to sabotage things with Colin."

"Sweetie, I know it was a horrible situation, but I really don't think that's what he was trying to do at all."

"What? What do you mean?" What did she mean?

"Look, you're upset. I completely understand. We'll go over it all when you get back to the city, okay?"

"But, Tess—"

"Lena?" Colin was calling from the other room.

"Oh Jesus. It's Colin. I have to go." I was frantic.

"Honey? Honey, are you listening to me?" Tess's voice was calm and instructive. "Just put it out of your mind. Everything's going to be just fine. We'll sort it all out together later."

"Thank you, Tess." I felt myself tear up again. What would I do without Tess, I wondered?

"Lena? Are you in there?" Colin tapped on the door lightly.

"Just one second." I quickly examined my face for evidence of crying. Luckily, it wasn't too obvious.

"Morning!" I said cheerily as I opened the bathroom door.

Colin smiled and, without a word, took me in his arms and kissed me. "Good morning to you," he said finally.

"Is everyone up yet?" I asked, resting my chin on his shoulder.

"No, they're all still sleeping, I think." He paused. "Except Cecily and Jake. They already headed back to the city."

At least I wouldn't have to face them this morning, I thought, relieved.

"Colin, about Jake—" I started, not sure what I intended to say.

"Yeah, what is with that guy?" Colin pulled away from me.

"Well, Jake's a complex person," I said, choosing my words carefully.

"I would say he's a complete asshole. I can't believe you two are friends," he said.

"Well, I know he was sort of...hostile...last night...." Why did I feel I needed to defend Jake all of a sudden?

"I'm just worried about Cecily, that's all," Colin said.

"I know, I understand. I am too, but—"

"I don't think she needs to be hanging around guys like that."

Guys like that? I felt my body tense. It was time to change the subject.

"What do you want to do today?"

"As if you don't know," he smiled at me playfully.

"I *don't* know. Tell me." I smiled back, wondering what adventure he had planned for us this time.

"I've got the final sit-down interview for your show to-morrow. We've got to start preparing!"

"Oh, right," I said. That wasn't at all the adventure I had hoped for.

chapter 9

The next day, when I arrived at the set for the sit-down interview, Colin was already there. He was deep into conversation with "the talent," Kelly Karaway. I sidled up beside him, preparing to introduce myself as if we'd never officially met. Our little secret was kind of fun.

"Hello, Mr. Bates. I'm Lena Sharpe, a producer for *Face to Face*."

"Oh, hey, Lena." Colin looked up at me distractedly. He seemed on edge, nervous. I guess that was natural—after all, he was being interviewed for the first time. He'd kept me up most of the night before with a long list of questions—wardrobe questions, technical questions, facial hair questions (should he shave and look responsible and clean-cut or go for a little stubble and try to pull off the renegade, dangerous author aesthetic). I noticed a sheen of product in his hair and he wore a shirt I hadn't seen before.

Kelly got up for another hair touch-up and I sat down across from him.

"Hey, how're you doing? It's going to be fine. They're just going to shoot some reaction shots now. We'll break for lunch and then start the interview." I fought the impulse to put my hand on his knee. "You'll be amazing. I know it."

"I'm not so sure. I'm really nervous."

"Well, I saw you were getting to know Kelly pretty well," I teased.

"Yeah, I was trying to get some of the questions out of her, but she wasn't taking the bait."

"Mmm…well, I'm afraid you're fishing in the wrong pond for starters."

"What?"

"Kelly doesn't have any clue what the questions are herself."

"She hasn't written them yet?"

"No," I laughed. "She doesn't write questions at all."

He looked at me blankly.

"Oh, Colin, I'm sorry to be the one to have to educate you about the eroding ideals of journalism, but I think Kelly's last gig was announcing lotto numbers on Channel Four."

"Well, who writes the questions?" He was getting worked up.

"Well, I do."

"*You* do? Are you serious?"

"I'm afraid so."

"I can't believe you never mentioned this before. Let me see!" He looked frantic.

"What? Are you serious?"

I looked at his face. He was serious.

"I can't do that, Colin. Come on."

"Why not?" He sounded like a petulant child.

"Why not? I just can't do that."

"You'd rather see me fuck up then?"

"You're not going to fuck up. This isn't *Nightline*. You'll be fine."

"Lena, this is a really big deal for me—this interview. I don't want to mess up. This is my first novel. Do you know how important that is?" He was more serious than I'd ever seen him before. And more vulnerable.

"I know. I—"

"Why wouldn't you want me to do well?"

"Colin, I—"

"I mean, it's not like I'm a war criminal or something, right?"

"Well, no…"

"Come on, Lena." He smiled at me sweetly now.

Fragments of an argument swirled in my head, but I couldn't quite fit them together. After all, he was right, on some level. This was a celebrity profile (or the closest thing to it when the subject isn't yet famous). I was starting to take my job as seriously as Nadine took hers. I could see his point and I could feel his sway pulling me. I placed the interview release form over my list of questions and handed them to him together. He smiled in reply.

"Colin, if you're ready, we're just going to shoot some close-ups of you," the director called to him from the control booth over the intercom.

"Ready as I'll ever be," he replied, winking at me.

I got up from Kelly's chair and made my way to the control room.

"Well, he's not what I expected." Nadine was behind me now. Cheese followed, as usual.

"What do you mean?" On second thought, I didn't really want to know what she meant.

"He's not the bookworm I had expected. You must be having a nice time with this one."

"Yes, he is telegenic," Cheese chimed in. Obviously he had learned a new word.

"He's very talented, actually," I said defensively.

"Oh, I bet he is." Nadine paused. "Just remember journalists must remain impartial." She gave me a knowing look—but *how* could she know? *What* did she know?—and walked away.

A few nights later, I met Colin for drinks at the bar at the Stanhope. I always found something alluringly clandestine about meeting at hotel bars. You know, forties film noir, Bogie and Bacall, that sort of thing. And this particular one had just the right warm, hazy lighting and vintage, mahogany feel. We passed a Sidecar back and forth between us, smoothing over the day's rough edges before we headed out for our night's events.

Colin and I had reached the stage where we were comfortable not talking all the time. Lately we seemed to be engaging in a lot of gazing—deep, meaningful gazing. (And thus I seemed to be engaging in a lot of deep, meaningful sighing).

"How was your day?" Colin stirred me from my reverie.

"Awful. Hellish. Completely ordinary."

"You've got to get out of that job."

"I know." We'd been through this same Q&A several times. He didn't need elaboration to know how much I wanted out of my job. "You?"

"Well, I had a lovely day of procrastination."

"So I've heard. In SoHo, I believe?"

"What?" He looked at me blankly.

"Caleb said you were headed to SoHo after you had lunch with him?"

"You talked to Caleb?" He seemed troubled by the idea. Was he jealous? How could he be jealous of Caleb? Not that I minded. A little masculine unease couldn't hurt.

"I had to messenger him his tickets for tonight, that's all." I smiled reassuringly, not unaware of the bizarreness inherent in my placating another person's insecurities.

"Is he coming?"

"Yeah, definitely. I think Grace and Gavin are coming, too."

The night's itinerary was a good one, even I had to admit. It was the opening night of the New York Film Festival—a black-tie, blue-blooded affair that kicked off the fall social season each year. More than two hundred carefully selected New Yorkers would eagerly spend at least two hours crammed into a hot screening room to see a highly anticipated, critically acclaimed and unbearably long film that would very likely never be spoken of again once the night was over. Essentially, it was a two-and-a-half hour excuse for a great after-party. Plus, I knew Tess and Parker would be there and I wanted to introduce them to Colin at long last.

"So, we'd better get going if we're going to make this screening," I said, glancing at my watch.

"What's the movie about again?" Colin asked.

"Something involving an Eskimo family. A character study, I believe." I paused. "You know, you keep asking me that question."

"I know. I keep hoping for a different answer." He smiled guiltily.

"Stop it—it sounds…edifying."

"Mmm, yes. So, I was thinking…why don't we just skip the screening and go straight to the party?" He looked at me mischievously.

"You're still playing hooky—all these years later."

"Look, people don't change."

"But how are we going to make idle chitchat about the film with all the other fabulous guests?"

"We'll just go on about subtext and metaphor—no one will know the difference, I promise."

"I don't know…Parker will kill me if our seats are left empty."

He paused and stared at me intently in a way that made me shift in my seat.

"You look amazing in that dress." He was smiling at me.

"Stop it, that's not going to work." I looked away but couldn't help blushing.

"Besides, this dress has been worn by at least four different women, I'm sure of it."

"I'm intrigued. Will they be joining us tonight?" He raised one eyebrow quizzically.

"It's vintage. Poor-girl chic, you know."

I was particularly proud of this acquisition—Yves Saint Laurent, circa 1968. I had engaged in a triumphant bidding war with a skinny French girl at Ina (and had won, I'm convinced, because her need for a cigarette finally wore her down. Ha!). In my fashion frenzy, I had blown my shoe budget and was forced to wear a pair of Tess's Ferragamo castoffs—one size too big, and thus stuffed with crumpled tissue at the toes. Classy, I know.

"My poor, sexy, sexy girl," Colin said, smiling sexily.

"And you know exactly what to say." I crinkled my toes inside my too-big shoes. He ran his fingers lightly over my hands.

"Is it working now?" He lowered his voice.

It was working.

★ ★ ★

Colin and I arrived at the party just after the first wave of guests had made it over from the screening. Everyone was polished and buffed, dermo-braised, lipo-ed, artificially bronzed, and hair plugged into place. There was the customary display of frantic cell phone dialing, bursts of over-enthusiastic conversations, and eager crowd-scanning all in the attempt to mask the insecurity of having been made to wait while the VIPs of the VIPs were ushered ahead without pause. Aside from the crowd's generous peppering of N.Y. filmmakers—complete with pasty faces and straggly goatees ("They're just pissed because they're poor and pale," as Parker would say, diplomatically), this was as L.A. as New York ever got.

Luckily I could see Parker, stationed at the door, fending off the crowd, clinically separating the connected and powerful from the very connected and very powerful. I took Colin's hand and made my way toward her. As only Parker could do amid such chaos, she reprimanded me for skipping the screening, gave Colin an approving once-over and warmly wished us a lovely time inside. In an instant, we were propelled forward by a swift tide of party-goers and deposited inside Shangri-la.

Okay, in reality it was Lot 61—a restaurant that most of these people had been to many, many times before. But a party was all about energy and name power and this one had both in spades. I looked around the room, each banquette was like a separate galaxy with its very own orbit of power—talent agents in this corner, studio chiefs in the other, etc. Colin grabbed two champagne flutes from a passing waiter as another stopped in front of us, bearing miniature Klondike bars, pricked with toothpicks for easy retrieval.

"I'm beginning to understand the theme here," Colin said, eyeing the polar treats. We giggled easily, aided by the succession of sidecars that we had happily consumed at the hotel.

"Oh, look there's an igloo ice sculpture at the bar." More giggling.

"Oh well, I guess Parker isn't really one for subtext and subtlety…oh wait, I see Tess."

In fact, what I did see was perhaps the most beautiful woman there, looking like an ice princess in a long, shimmering white column dress—which was only outdone by the string of diamonds resting nonchalantly around her neck. Ah, Tess.

Tess's arm was linked around her date for the evening. Apparently Stanley had fallen off her list—too wrapped up in some merger and acquisition matter. So Tess had diverged and made a new acquisition of her own. His name was Dalton and he was similar to most of her men—older, rich, distinguished, well-mannered, and hopelessly Waspy. I was half convinced that all of Tess's paramours were very likely related if one traced back the lineage far enough.

"Pleased to meet you, I'm Dalton."

"I'm Lena. And this is…"

"Hey there, Colin. Good to see you again. How've you been?"

"I've been okay, Dalt. Thanks."

They knew each other? Obviously. But neither elaborated and something in the air between them told me not to inquire. An awkward foot shuffle and silence ensued. I felt suddenly sober.

I searched for something to fill the space. "Tess, you look so great. Is that your Dior?"

"It's actually Christian Lacroix," Dalt piped in.

"Well, you have excellent taste Mr…I mean Dalton." I could feel Tess tense and I was sorry for the mistake. It *was* a mistake.

"Hey, everyone!" Parker had arrived on the scene, thank God.

"Is everyone having a good time?" She didn't wait for a response. "I'm so glad! Al Pacino just stopped me to rave about the polar-bear claws. Isn't that just the best!"

"Parker, I haven't formally introduced you. This is Colin Bates," I said.

"It's a pleasure." She batted her eyes as only Parker could.

"And this is Dalton Fulham," Tess joined in.

"Lovely to meet you both. Now excuse me, just one second, but I need to talk to my girls for a moment." Parker herded us away from the boys toward the bar.

"What was going on there?" I looked at Tess.

"No idea, but I don't think we'll be spending the evening together."

"Um, I'll tell you what was going on there—are you telling me that neither of you know?" Parker looked at us incredulously.

We both stared at her blankly, as we often did.

"Your date—" she looked at Tess "—used to date your date's—" she turned her head to me "—mother."

"Oh my…" Tess began.

"God." I finished.

Tess and I looked at each other, not sure what to say. I felt vaguely guilty for putting Colin in this situation. And I felt a certain annoyance with Tess for putting me in this situation. And then I felt guilty because I knew Tess hadn't knowingly put me in this situation. And I also felt annoyance at Parker for enjoying the fact that she was the one to reveal this information. Guilt and annoyance.

"How do you know this for sure?" Of course, Tess's cynicism always kicked in first.

"My assistant Blair's older brother used to play rugby with one of Dalt's old girlfriend's stepsons. She slipped me a note when she saw you guys talking."

"Why should we trust your staff's gossip ring?"

"Um, I got a confirmation before I came over here, Tess. I've got two interns whose mothers know Colin's mom from Doubles."

"Any other details we should be aware of?"

"Well, it's not like I went digging. I *am* trying to run a party here, girls. Speaking of which, I think the Hilton sisters are going to try to hop on the bar. I've got to go."

"Well, I guess I'm just going to have to keep my guy away from your guy," I said.

"Guess so," Tess said, not backing down.

We were both annoyed, that was clear. I'd have time for guilt later.

I made my way back over to Colin, who by that time had extricated himself from Dalt and was trading business cards with an older, bespectacled man who looked familiar, but I couldn't quite place.

"It is such a thrill to meet you, really," I could hear Colin say as I got closer. "Honestly, *Writer's Roundtable* is all I watch anymore. I can't tell you how inspirational it is."

"Good to hear, Colin. Listen, I'll definitely be in touch." The older man shook Colin's hand enthusiastically and headed for the bar.

"Who was that?" I asked, coming up beside Colin.

"That was Walt Colmby," Colin answered happily.

"Oh, from that PBS show. I knew he looked familiar. That guy is so obnoxious."

"I know, I can't stand him," Colin agreed.

"You just said his show was inspirational!" I said.

"Lena, dear, the man might be an imbecile, but his show sells books. You've got to play the game a little," he said, scanning the crowd.

"Hey." I touched him on the shoulder. "I'm so sorry about that run-in with Tess's date earlier."

"Dalt used to date my mom. Just so you know."

"I know. Parker just told me. I hope it wasn't too awkward."

"No big deal. Happens all the time. New York's a small town in a lot of ways. We'll just keep moving."

"Sounds good to me," I said.

We shared a smile and I grabbed his hand to make our way through the crowd. Just as I turned, however, I suddenly found a familiar face planted in front of me—Jake. New York was a small town, indeed.

He looked first at me, wordlessly, and then shifted his gaze toward Colin, offering only a cool once-over. It was our first meeting since that infamous night a couple weeks earlier. I hadn't known what to say to him—and I still didn't, even with him standing right in front of me.

I paused, looking at Jake, trying to get a read on just how rude he intended to be. He appeared to be alone—Cecily was certainly nowhere in sight. No doubt, he had already moved on to someone else.

"How are you, Lena?" he asked.

"I'm okay. Busy." I paused. "How are you?"

It was like a conversation between two former co-workers who happened to run into each other on a subway platform.

"I'll be fine," he said and, after a brief pause, he turned and walked away.

"Jake—"

I moved to follow him, but Colin grabbed my hand. I watched him as he slowly disappeared into the crowd.

"This night really isn't off to a great start," I said to Colin once I had recovered. "I wonder where Gavin and those guys are anyway?" I looked around the room, searching for friendly faces. Nothing.

"Aw, fuck 'em—we were having more fun before we got here, anyway." Colin bent down and kissed my neck. Maybe it was time to go, I thought.

"Lena?"

I couldn't place the voice immediately, but I did feel a visceral shiver. When I turned my head, I saw none other than Sleazy Cheese standing before me. The whole room was turning into a funhouse, with a newer, bigger, scarier monster lurking at every turn.

He looked all of twelve years old in his rent-a-tux and shellacked hair. He held two martinis and sipped thirstily from one. He was obviously thrilled with his discovery.

"Oh, hi, Chase. I didn't expect to see you here."

"Guess not." He was beaming now, looking directly at Colin. Dammit, dammit, dammit.

"Chase, you remember Colin." I tried to sound nonchalant. It's not like I couldn't talk to another guest at a party, after all.

"Oh yes, I remember." Cheese smiled.

Chase, it seemed, had in fact grasped the idea of subtext. If there had been any question as to whether the little runt would run right back to Mama to tell on me, his positively giddy expression provided the answer. In fact, the only thing I could imagine that would take his mind off the utter glee of having been admitted to this power-packed room would be to rat on me to Nadine. He was the principal and Colin and I were the two kids making out in the bathroom.

"I didn't realize you two knew each other on a personal level," Cheese said with an exaggerated wink.

I ignored the question, but Cheese's attention had suddenly been diverted.

"Nadine! There you are!" Cheese waved wildly. As if on cue, Nadine appeared out of nowhere, a swirl of smoke and sequins. She took Chase's other martini.

"Well, hello, Lena," Nadine smiled slowly at me. "I didn't expect to see you here. Have you been plucking invitations from my mail again?"

I looked at her, the layers of foundation spackled on her aging face, the gross abuse of body shimmer that made her look like a roller-skating queen circa 1976. I didn't know what to say or how to proceed. I knew she wanted me to explain why Colin and I were together, to put me on the spot and exert her authority in front of her little lover.

"Hi, Nadine. You remember Colin, don't you?"

"Oh, I do, indeed."

"Nice to see you again." Colin looked dazed at this point.

"Lena." Nadine held her eyes on Colin. "I'm afraid I have a problem here."

"What's the problem, Nadine?"

"Well, dear…" She looked me in the eye now. "I'm not sure how this arrangement is going to work for us."

"This arrangement?"

"Yes." Her eyes moved lazily from Colin and then rested on me.

"I'm not sure what you mean."

"One needs to be aware of appearances in this business," she said icily.

"I'm still not quite clear what you're speaking of." I let my eyes wander from Cheese and then back to Nadine.

There was a pause and then she said, "I mean you can't be fucking the guests, sweetheart. No matter how cute they are." She smiled.

I don't think I had ever hated Nadine more than I did in that moment. I felt every petty comment, every last-minute job dumped on my lap, every stolen achievement and verbal slight, every obnoxious Post-it, every single ounce of strength that I had used to stave off my Nadine rage, to rise above, to keep perspective, and to persevere collide together, igniting one unstoppable, brilliant flash of rage.

"Nadine, you and your little man-child can go fuck yourselves."

The first thing I noticed was Cheese's face, which had turned an ashen white. And then I saw that Colin had frozen in place sort of like a statue. Things were in slow motion, as I might have imagined, and I felt my body set itself in a self-defense posture, as if I expected to be punched. Really, at that point anything was possible.

I found myself staring back at Nadine, who looked as if she were just recovering from a severe blow to the head. I wondered what would come next, but not in a frantic, worried way. Even in my shock, I knew what I had said—and I didn't care. I would not plead Not Guilty by Reason of Insanity. No, I'd done the deed and there was no turning back. I felt strangely calm. Not heroic or validated or triumphant—just peaceful and calm—similar to the feeling of well-being one often assumes after vomiting.

At least things were clear now—sides had been chosen. A moment in which one chooses to hurl epithets at one's boss is not a moment rife with shades of gray.

"You are so fucking fired, Sharpe." Nadine bellowed the

words in a martini-saliva spray. I could feel the crowd pause for a moment, examine our status, and then return to their business upon noting the low gossip quotient.

It was time to go.

chapter 10

The next morning was not what I had always imagined it would be. You see, I had given a great deal of thought to just exactly what this morning would be like—my first day of freedom. Of course, last night was not how I imagined my last day on the job would be, either.

It was supposed to have been a graceful exit. I would have a farewell dinner, or at least a gathering for drinks at a swanky bar. Perhaps the Royalton or the Paramount—something symbolically equivalent to my ascension into the elite media hierarchy. I would wear Armani, of course, black with a few well chosen pieces of jewelry and unforgiving stilettos elevating me heads above the rest. I would nurse a flute of champagne while a stream of network executives and fellow producers crowded around me wishing me well, subtly palming me their business cards as they looked pleadingly into my eyes, mentally begging that I take them with me, remember them, come back and save them from this sorry life. My departure would have been the subject of water-cooler chat for days—ever since I had called a meeting with the E.P. (bypassing Nadine, of course) to let them know I'd be leaving. Of course, there were counteroffers, grand sums of money and luxurious perks casually mentioned during a steady succession of expense account lunches at the Four Seasons. But with the three-book contract and the TV development deal, it was just sort of sad really. My parting words would be wise and philosophical. I would offer kind words for those with whom I'd toiled, great optimism for our collective futures, and just a few, ever so subtle yet excoriating digs at Nadine. But she didn't matter all that much anymore—her days were numbered given that she had let a talent like me slip through the network's grasp. I would float above the masses, untouchable as I was already half-gone, catapulted ahead toward stratospheric professional success.

Instead, I found myself swimming up from sleep, facing the fact that I had no job, no source of income, no hope for a recommendation. What I did have was one brutal hangover. Pieces from the night before were beginning to realign in my head. Leaving the party. Running out with Colin behind me. I remembered a bar—and drinks—and then a diner and fluorescent lights, and finally—oh-so-vividly—a toilet, my toilet. So I *had* made it home. Colin wasn't around, but my clothes were off.

I didn't have the energy to get up. No, it was worse than that—I couldn't imagine having the energy to get up ever again. It wasn't supposed to be this way, no. But even though things had gone completely astray from my mental game plan, I still couldn't help but be glad that I would never ever have to go back to that job again.

I heard the latch on my door open and Colin appeared,

carrying a brown paper bag. He smiled at me and sat down on the edge of the bed.

"Good morning," he said finally, and handed me an ice-cold bottle of Poland Spring and two aspirin tablets.

"My hero," I said huskily, and drank from the bottle.

"That was quite a night you had, young lady."

"So there's no chance that I might have just been asleep for the past twenty-four hours, huh?"

"I'm afraid not."

"Oh Jesus, what have I done?" I fell back on my bed and covered my face with my hands.

"Well, you got quite a bit done, if you must know."

"I'm an idiot."

"You're not an idiot. Nadine's an idiot. Cheese is an even bigger idiot."

"True. But they're idiots with discernible sources of income."

"You hated that job. You were dying to leave."

"I know, but this isn't how it was supposed to happen."

"Look, you're better off just putting *Face to Face* behind you. I'm telling you, after my segment airs, we are never watching that show again."

"Assuming they still go ahead and air it after last night's drama," I said, pulling a pillow over my face.

"What? What do you mean?" Colin sounded concerned.

"I'm just saying, I can totally see Nadine doing something like that. Just for spite," I said.

"Wait? Are you really serious?" Colin was definitely concerned.

I pulled the pillow off my face. "What's wrong? Are you upset?"

"No, no, I'm not thinking about me." He sat up a little straighter. "I was just thinking of all that work that you did."

"You're so sweet," I said, but I still sensed that he was tense. "I'm just being cynical, though. Even Nadine doesn't have the authority to pull it off the schedule at this point," I said reassuringly. "Besides, your uncle will make sure it airs."

"You're right. I'd better give him a call. Okay, no more work talk," Colin said, clearly feeling better. "You know, I was thinking this morning that we should take a trip. Do a little exploring now that you've got some free time." He looked at me expectantly and then his eyes lit up. "We'll go to West Virginia! How about a little white-water rafting?"

I again realized how different our worlds were—how a month or two to "explore" was a natural occurrence for Colin, and a parallel universe for me. But he made me feel I was part of his world and that maybe it was possible for me, too. And I liked that. For a second, I began to believe that things really would be okay.

Until that is, I talked to anyone else. Of course, there was sympathy and compassion—but these kind words were inevitably followed by a painful pause and then the question: What do you think you're going to do?

This time it was Tess posing the question, as we sat down for tea on her terrace.

"Well, I've been thinking about my skills."

"Yeah?" Tess sounded hopeful.

"And I've realized that I have none."

"That's not true. You just need to get out there and start looking."

"You know, I'm actually quite happy not doing anything at all. The hamster wheel that was my life has stopped and I feel fine. Things finally feel a little peaceful."

"You're awfully philosophical today," Tess said.

"It's just that I guess I always felt a little guilty dating Colin on the sly. Maybe, in some ways, I deserved to get fired," I said pensively.

"Lena, you don't have anything to feel guilty about. You gave way more to that show than it gave to you. Besides, Nadine's dating her assistant, isn't she?"

"Yeah," I said.

"I rest my case."

"You know, maybe it's just too much to ask to have everything at once—personal *and* professional satisfaction." I felt a mini-epiphany coming on. "Maybe I should just enjoy my relationship and be happy for a while."

"Lena, that's a beautiful idea, but you need to be realistic. Your relationship isn't going to pay your rent."

"You're such a downer."

"So you've told me about five thousand times. By the way, how are you with money? Let me know if you need anything, okay?"

"Thanks, Tess."

"And promise me…" She paused. "That you'll ask me before you ask him."

"I'm not asking anyone."

We sat there silent for a moment.

"Lena, have you talked to Jake at all?"

"No," I said brusquely. "Have *you?*"

"Well, I ran into him a few days ago on the street."

"Really?" I tried to feign mild curiosity, as if we were talking about a former acquaintance of mine, perhaps someone from the gym.

"I know we haven't really talked about what happened in Easthampton."

"Because there's nothing to talk about."

"Okay," Tess said, willing to drop the subject.

"You don't agree?" I guess I wasn't quite ready to let it go.

"I think…" Tess chose her words carefully now. "I think he was trying to tell you something and he went about it in the wrong way."

"I can't believe you're taking his side," I said, even though I knew she wasn't.

"I'm not, Lena. I'm really not."

Silence.

"So, what did he say? Jake, I mean." I hated that I wanted to know. I hated that I had to ask.

"We talked about his new gallery. He's meeting with a bunch of new artists. Stuff like that."

More silence.

"How did he seem?"

Tess thought for a moment. "Sad," she said finally. "He seemed sad."

And then the subject was closed. There really wasn't anything left to say.

"I might go to West Virginia with Colin." The words came out quickly, as if I wanted to erase the previous discussion topic.

"What?" Tess put down her teacup without taking a sip. "You're going where?"

"We might take a trip together."

"You're going to West Virginia with Colin?"

"Yeah, I think we're going to go white-water rafting. Absorb nature. Just spend some time alone. It's nice knowing he wants to be with me, you know."

"Well, I guess I can't argue with that, can I?"

"Finally, you're going to trust me? I win?"

"You win, Lena. You win."

When Parker arrived at French Roast, I was cozily ensconced in a corner table, surrounded by the Sunday paper, which I had almost entirely read for a change. My days now consisted largely of caffeinated beverages and reading material. I wasn't complaining.

"Gee, I didn't realize that you'd set up an office here."

"Very funny. Actually, Colin was here earlier, but he went for a run and I've just been going through the paper. What's up?" Parker had made one of her frantic phone calls, imploring a group meeting ASAP.

"Where's Tess?"

"She's on her way. She just called from a cab."

"Okay, I'll wait." She sat down impatiently, clearly about to burst with the excitement of her secret.

"Parker, are you okay?"

"No, I can't wait. It's too much. I'll just tell her later."

Now, Parker always had a story she was dying to tell, some nugget of fresh gossip that she had picked up from one of her many sources and which would mercilessly preoccupy her until she had delivered it to a hungry audience. Only then could she exhale and go on about her business.

"Parker, what is it?" I settled in for what would very likely be another scandalous story involving her arch enemy, rival publicist Sissy Leventhal.

Parker leaned forward in her seat. Her cheeks were red and her eyes were watering with what could have been either tears of joy or sadness. I couldn't tell which.

"Oh honey…" She was crying in earnest now. "It's about you."

"Me?"

At that moment, Tess walked in and, even in my state of confusion with Parker, I could tell she had just refreshed her lipstick in preparation for a possible encounter with Macho Macchiato.

"Parker, what's wrong?" Tess asked.

"Lena's getting married," Parker declared with glee.

"What?" Tess and I blurted out at the same time. Somehow, this was not how I'd imagined my engagement announcement.

"You're what?" Tess looked at me, confused.

"I'm what?" I looked at Parker, confused.

"Okay, I should explain."

"Yeah, I think you really should," Tess said, taking a seat.

"Well, you know how Brad and I have been arguing over wedding bands?" Parker began.

Tess and I nodded vigorously.

"He likes—"

"Tiffany's," Tess said.

"And I like—"

"Harry Winston," I finished.

"And no matter how many times I've tried to explain to him that the only people who would think to buy a wedding ring from Tiffany's are—"

"Tourists—" Tess began.

"Or new money," I finished.

"Okay, I guess I did tell you guys that story already. Anyway…"

"Sorry to interrupt you there, Parker, but could we possibly get to the part about me, well, getting married?"

"I'm getting there," Parker said haughtily. She did not like to rush her stories.

"Well, we compromised," Parker smiled proudly as if it were now clear that her marriage was clearly built to last the stormy tides of matrimony that had wrecked so many other unions.

"You see, I found this verrrry exclusive jeweler in SoHo that custom-designs engagement rings and wedding bands."

She paused. "You won't find Marsden rings in the pages of *In Style,* let's be clear."

"Okay, I'm still not following." Even Tess was getting impatient.

Parker looked at me with deep, meaningful eyes. For a second, I thought *she* might propose.

"I saw Colin there."

"You did?"

She nodded, her eyes closed. She touched my hand. "Oh honey."

"What did he say?"

"He didn't see me! I ducked into the patisserie next door when I saw him through the window." She smiled. "I'm quick like that. I didn't want to ruin his surprise, after all."

"Well, Parker—if it is true…" Tess began.

"Oh, it is true, Tess."

"Then it's not going to be much of a surprise for Lena, is it?"

"Surprise?" Parker spit the words out. "Oh please! I don't want to deprive poor Colin from his little moment, but a woman—" she started a new declaration "—should not be surprised by a proposal. A woman should look ravishing and be dressed in a matrimonially acceptable way. She should be composed, yet exhilarated. A woman should not, however, be *surprised*. Who knows what might happen then? She might choke on her food or knock over her wine. She might be suffering from menstrual cramps or be wearing something she's worn before."

"Okay, let's all calm down. Nothing conclusive has happened." I was suddenly the voice of reason. Yet in my head or, I should say, in my heart, I could feel a twitch, a shift— could it be true?

Yes, I could see it so clearly…

It would be in Vermont, at a quaint chapel in the country. Not a huge affair, but a careful selection of our dearest family members and friends. My dress would be elegant and superbly tailored. Something deceptively simple that would likely influence bridal trends for years to come once the pictures inevitably ended up in *Town and Country*. I would wear one of Colin's grandmother's jewels that his mother would give to me one day unexpectedly, with a tear in her eye and a hushed monologue on how blessed she felt to have me in the family. My eyes would gleam, my hair would shine, and my pores would be invisible. We would write our own vows—Colin would quote Keats and I would reference Tennyson. There would be the requisite moment of matrimonial levity—a prolonged kiss by the groom, perhaps— inspiring laughter from an approving audience. Afterward, we would have our reception at a small bed-and-breakfast, with guests spilling outside (of course, the weather would be beautiful) to lounge on hay bales as they sipped champagne to the sounds of crickets. At some point, Colin would whisk me away from the parade of well-wishers to the back terrace where he would tell me again how lucky he was to have me and how much he loved me. And we would stay there together, alone under the stars.

On the way home, I found myself noticing the fingers of everyone I encountered. I was astounded by the number of rings I saw—gold, silver and platinum spheres, all shining their significance proudly. Some nested snugly with sparkling engagement rings, others stood alone, simple and solitary. They were everywhere. Bare hands suddenly looked empty, insignificant, naked. I rubbed my own empty finger and considered what it might feel like to have a ring of my own, to announce to the world, silently but resolutely, that

I was not available for sideward glances, lame chitchat, get-to-know-you brunches, or quick and painful meet-for-a-drink auditions. Could I possibly be finally, completely—legitimately—spoken for? I breathed a sigh of relief.

I took a detour by the green market to buy flowers and fresh vegetables. Ah, domesticity! Through the gauzy lens of my new tranquility, my life started to make sense. One chapter had closed (work) just as another had opened (Colin). In fact, work and all its misery had brought Colin to me. The suffering now made sense. In this light, Colin could be seen as the just reward for so much heartache and frustration. It had not all been for naught.

Once at home, I quickly and happily prepared a vibrant salad. It's amazing what figuring out your future in the span of an afternoon can inspire. I even made croutons!

I reached for the phone. I so wanted to talk to Jake—he had always been my reflexive first phone call when either something wonderful or terrible happened to me. My good mood ran cold when I thought of our last interaction. The phone rang with my hand still on it.

"Hello?"

"Hey, Lena." It was Colin. I felt myself beaming.

"Listen, I'm going to be stuck here with Knox for a while so I don't think dinner's going to work."

Knox was Colin's editor and, for some reason, always seemed to prefer doing business late into the night. I had started calling him "Knox-turnal." The two were deep in the throes of editing Colin's second novel, so last-minute cancellations were *de rigeur* these days.

"Okay." I was a little disappointed. My new information made me anxious to see him again, to observe his behavior. It was sort of like that feeling when you buy a new pair of shoes to go with an outfit and you can't wait to see how it looks—on a much grander, more meaningful scale, of course.

"We'll have the whole weekend together, though," he said. "Does that sound good?"

We'll have our whole lives, I thought. "That sounds great, Colin," I said.

"You know, they say it's a sign of adulthood when a young woman buys a matching set of luggage."

"Really?" I said, considering that idea for a second before continuing to try to shed the perky saleswoman who had been shadowing me ever since I made the mistake of lingering too long in front of a Jerome Gruet carry-on.

"Well, I'm not a girl," I teased her, "but I'm not yet a woman, either." I headed directly to the Samsonite section. "As Britney likes to say."

I hadn't meant to be shopping. In fact, I was on my way to mail my application for unemployment, but the magnetic pull of consumerism had won out over that somber task for the time being. Besides, all I had in the way of luggage was a battered backpack that had been dragged through one too many European youth hostels.

"And where will you be traveling?" Jeez, she would not give up. Salespeople had to be the only New Yorkers that always seemed starved for conversation.

"West Virginia," I said flatly.

She looked at me quizzically, pursing her lips as if she'd just smelled sour milk or perhaps seen a vinyl attaché.

That did it, I smiled to myself.

"Excuse me." I had to beg for the clerk's attention now.

"Yes," she said distractedly.

"Do you know where the closest post office is?"

"Two blocks down on the right," she informed me without turning around. "Next to Marsden."

"Marsden?" I said the name quietly. Reverently.

"It's a jewelry store." The clerk turned to me, peering over her glasses. "But it's very high end."

"Thanks," I smiled. "I know."

It was a quaint little town house, painted slate-blue with an iron gate. A small gold plaque discreetly inscribed "Marsden" announced its identity. My heart skipped a beat.

I rang the bell and, after a few moments, the door buzzed open. No one was in sight. The decor was spare and modern, the space completely silent except for the subtle buzz of the air conditioner. I walked slowly toward the granite counter and peered down at the selection of precious metal before me. A strange calmness washed over me as if I were in church.

The door buzzed open again and my reverie was interrupted by a well-dressed couple with expectant eyes and intertwined hands. They were obviously swirling happily in the giddy, unreal haze of premarital planning. Dating was a lot like swimming with sharks and engaged couples always seemed to have the slightly dazed glee of having made it out of the water before being maimed. The couple walked with purpose toward the counter—it was time to claim their prize. A salesman appeared, wearing a black Nehru-collared coat and a superior expression.

"May I help you?" he asked me sourly.

"I'm just browsing, really." Does one ordinarily "browse" for wedding rings? And then to cover, asked, "Do you sell other types of jewelry?" Of course then, I stopped short, realizing that I might have asked a question that I didn't want to know the answer to. After all, maybe they sold money clips, business-card holders. Maybe Colin was here buying a new key fob.

"No."

"Oh good!" I breathed a sigh of relief.

"Excuse me, I have a question," the well-dressed man interrupted us. He looked like the kind of man who generally got his questions answered quickly. The salesman abandoned me, rushing to his aid. The three conferred in somber tones about platinum settings.

"Actually, the designer is in the store today," Nehru-collared man said in a way that made it sound as if all who were present were very, very fortunate.

"Malena, could you come out here for a second?"

A swift kick in the stomach was the sensation that followed. The ghost from Colin's past had returned, this time in the form of a beautiful high-end jeweler. She emerged from the back room looking as ethereal and luminescent as the wedding bands she sold.

"You had a question?" She addressed the couple politely.

The well-dressed man's face softened in the way that it does when a man sees a beautiful woman. I guess even the giddiness of engagement can't cancel that out.

"You're Malena Marsden?" I heard myself ask in a voice several octaves higher than normal.

The well-dressed couple, Nehru-collared man and the beautiful designer all turned to look at me.

"Do we know each other?" Malena Marsden looked at me again, searching for some sense of familiarity. My mind stalled as I stamped out my knee-jerk tendency to answer questions honestly. I mean, in a sense, I did know her.

"Oh, I must have read about you in a magazine." They continued to stare. "I think maybe it was *In Style.*"

The group's collective look of confusion suddenly gave way to condescending laughter.

"Um, I'm sorry, dear, but Malena would never appear in *In Style,*" Nehru-collared man sniffed.

I found myself mumbling an apology and shuffling out the door like a homeless woman kicked out of a fancy restaurant. I could hear the faint lilt of laughter inside. I was alone now, left only with the detritus of my former fantasy.

"Colin, I need to talk to you," I said out loud finally. The words, planned fifteen blocks or so earlier when I had found myself walking directly toward Knox's office, had been festering ever since. It felt good to set them free.

"Lena?" Colin sat up from his reclined position across from Knox's desk. The two were eating Chinese food in his office—pages of what I assumed to be Colin's new manuscript were strewn about, bloodied with red edit marks. I had burst through the door moments earlier, every bit the living embodiment of a woman scorned. I cringed at the cliché—I could easily be reenacting the climactic scene of just about any Lifetime movie at that moment. Wordlessly, Knox slipped out of the room.

"What are you talking about? What's going on?" He seemed truly baffled.

"Malena," I said firmly.

"What?"

I stood silent.

He looked small and frail in his chair. An errant lo mein noodle stuck to his left pant leg.

"What about her?"

"I know what's going on, Colin."

"Lena, you're not making sense."

"Don't make me spell this out for you. It's hard enough as it is."

When I had envisioned this confrontation, I hadn't really planned for follow-up questions.

"I don't know what you're talking about. Help me here."

Help him?

"Parker saw you at Marsden. I was just there. *I* saw her. *Malena Marsden.* God, I'm so stupid." I shook my head, which must have triggered the tears, because they soon followed.

"Malena is just an old friend of mine, Lena."

"Oh, I know. Vanessa made that very clear." Her words rang in my head. *"First loves run deep." "Are you a jealous person, Lena?"*

"You're basing all this on something Vanessa said?"

"It's not just Vanessa." There had been so many signs. Or there had seemed to be. Everything that had been so certain in my head now seemed tenuous and circumstantial when said out loud.

"I saw her. I *know* you were there." The golden vision of Malena still haunted me.

"Do you even realize what you're saying to me? Think about this, Lena." His words were slow and steady, as if I were standing on a ledge, threatening to jump.

"Colin, I—"

"I know you have a vivid imagination, but suddenly I'm cheating on you because I went to visit an old friend?"

"She's an old *girlfriend,* Colin," I corrected him.

Colin paused for a moment and then bent down, reaching into his bag. He pulled out an ivory envelope and handed it to me wordlessly.

"Read it," he said.

Reluctantly I pulled out the card inside:

"Malena Chapman Marsden and Raphael Esteban Consuelos III, together with their parents, Edward Mann and Mary Elizabeth Marsden and Enrique and Raquel Consuelos request the honor of your presence at their wedding…"

What had I done?

"This is not the way to have a trusting relationship, Lena."

"Colin, I just thought—"

"You just thought you would come in here in the middle of the day and hurl accusations at me. Is that it?"

"Colin, I'm so sorry." And I was.

"You have to trust me Lena or—"

"I trust you, Colin, I trust you." Now he was the one on the ledge and I was trying to coax him down. I moved in closer, putting my arms around him, holding on to him. He didn't move away, but he didn't move toward me, either. "I'm so sorry."

"You've got to trust me, Lena. There's no other way." I thought—I hoped—that his voice had softened.

"I know. I do. I'm sorry."

"There's no other way."

"I just get these ideas and—"

"I know you do, I know." He was comforting me now.

The drama had passed. The fire engines pulled away. Show's over.

chapter 11

"So, you're not getting married then?" Parker asked, dis-appointedly. "I was so sure of it."

"That sort of misses the point, Parker," Tess said sharply, and then turned to me. "Oh, Lena, I can't believe what you've just been through. I'm sorry." She looked as devas-tated as I felt. The three of us were piled on Tess's bed like teenagers at a slumber party.

I had just finished describing the horrible drama to them in such exhaustive detail that I felt I had relived the whole ordeal all over again. I curled myself into a fetal position and wondered what would happen if I stayed like that forever.

"If you could have just seen me, I was hysterical," I said, still trying to process what had happened.

"Of course you were. I would have been the same way," Tess sympathized.

"I don't blame you. You were in shock," Parker added.

In my head, I could see Tess and Parker listening to me,

nodding their heads and offering their support. But I was still numb. I had seen my world sway out of focus and then right itself again. Or had it? A heart-to-heart with the girls wasn't going to salve the wound this time.

"I can't even believe he's still talking to me," I said.

"Most guys wouldn't, that's true," Parker said flatly.

Tess glared at Parker. "You made a mistake, Lena. That's all."

"She's right though, Tess. He's being great, which makes me feel so much worse. I feel like *I* betrayed him," I said.

"Just spoil him for a little while. He'll get over it," Parker counseled.

"How did I become this person? It's like I'm the worst cliché of a jealous woman ever," I groaned.

"This will pass. Things will go back to normal," Tess advised.

"Will they?" I desperately wanted to believe her, but I wasn't so sure. "He doesn't trust me. How could he? What do we have if we don't have trust?"

It was a Saturday afternoon, a few weeks after "the Malena incident," and I sat with Colin, Caleb and Gavin in the back corner booth at Fanelli's. They had just finished a game of soccer in the park and now everyone was settled in for a long stretch of drinking and hanging out. I could honestly say that by this point, things between Colin and I *had* in fact gone back to normal—were it not for the unrelenting throb of guilt that continued to plague me, of course.

"Hey, guys," Colin said as he got up from the table, "I'm going to put some money in the jukebox. Enough of this boy-band shit already."

"And I'm going to go ask our waitress why she gave me a Jack and Coke without the Jack," Gavin said, heading for the bar.

"You're starting to sound like me," Caleb called out to him, giving me a sly wink.

"So, Ms. Lena, what's new with you?" he asked, now that it was just the two of us.

I wondered for a moment if he knew about my confrontation with Colin. "Not too much," I said, shaking off the thought. "Still woefully unemployed, I'm afraid."

"See, now we have something in common!" he said, sounding truly delighted.

"That's right, we can pound the pavement together," I said.

"Oh no, no, there will be none of that," he said, looking pained. "There's so much cool stuff to be done while everyone else is working. The park is empty, the stores are empty. Oh, you know what we should do next week—" he exclaimed, accidentally knocking his Budweiser all over his sweatshirt.

"Nice one. Are you drunk already?" Colin called out from the other side of the bar.

"It's all Lena's fault," Caleb kidded me as he lifted up his arms to take off his beer-soaked shirt.

"Yeah, right—" I started to say, but caught myself mid-sentence.

"Lena," Caleb laughed. "You look like you just saw a ghost."

There it was. Just above his elbow, in the same clumsy writing and the same faded blue ink.

"We met this sailor and he was going to tattoo our girlfriends' names on our arms, but he mixed them up."

"Lena. What's wrong?" Caleb was speaking to me, but my mind was somewhere else. Thinking. Remembering. Bits and fragments of conversations from the past, pieces of a jigsaw puzzle that held all the answers.

"Your tattoo—it's just like Colin's," I said, doing my best to feign normalcy.

"Whose name was it supposed to be?" "Her name was Lena."
He smiled. "That's the only name I can think of right now."

"Are you okay?" Caleb asked cautiously.

I didn't answer. This cannot be happening again, I thought.

"I don't think she should be hanging around guys like Jake. I'll talk to her."

"I don't know. Should I be?"

"What?" He was confused.

"Should I be okay?" I was direct, focused.

"Of course. It's just that you looked upset."

"You know what's going on, Caleb, don't you?"

He didn't answer. He didn't have to. His eyes told me everything I needed to know.

"Cecily's always been special."

"How long has it been going on?" I asked.

"God, I'm sorry, Lena." And I could tell that he was.

"Just tell me. I want to know."

Caleb lowered his eyes. "High school. It just never really ended. I thought maybe it would when she started dating your friend, Jake, but I think she was just trying to make him jealous."

"You just come here in the middle of the day hurling accusations at me. This is not the way to have a trusting relationship, Lena."

"Caleb, you're a good person," I said, rising from the table. "It's not your fault that your best friend is a complete and total asshole."

"Lena." It was Colin. He was smiling like an idiot, pointing to the stereo speaker, which had just begun piping out the opening strains of "Stand By Me." "May I have this dance?" he said, approaching the table. Then he saw my face. "What's wrong?"

"Everything," I said flatly.

He looked confused. Caleb had buried his head in his hands, preparing for the inevitable.

"Apparently, my imagination isn't as misleading as you'd like to have me believe."

"I don't know what you're talking about." He looked at me and then at Caleb.

Caleb didn't answer; he just shook his head in defeat.

"That seems to be your favorite refrain, Colin." I paused. "And I'm sure Cecily will be hearing it before too long."

"Lena, you are not going to start this again." His voice was threatening.

"No, I'm not," I looked at Caleb and then back to Colin. "A man more honest than you just finished it."

Moments later, I collapsed in a window booth at Veselka. Tears slid messily down my face, but I didn't bother to wipe them away. It was still too early for the dinner rush and the place was nearly empty. A portly Ukrainian woman with flesh-colored panty hose and dyed white-blond hair tied up in an Ivana-esque twist approached with a menu and a glass of water.

"Thank you," I said.

She gently patted my hand and smiled. "Svetlana," her name tag read in all caps.

I sipped my water and waited. What had just happened? What was going to happen next? I had immediately called Tess after I left Fanelli's and she had calmly instructed me to wait here until she arrived. It was a place I knew well. I used to come here every weekend when I lived across the street. I only lived a few blocks away now, but it felt like I was visiting a different city, a different life. Through the window, I could even see my old building and, if I hunched down a bit, the window to my first apartment in New York.

It had been a snowy March day (a fluke spring snowstorm, they had said) when I pulled up in a cab to that very building with one suitcase, a couple hundred dollars, and what now seems to have been an alarming sense of optimism. I had finished college the previous spring and had spent the ensuing time battling between the practical and the romantic. The romantic won out and thus I packed everything up and moved to New York.

That first night I couldn't sleep, but not because I didn't yet have a mattress and was using my coat as a pillow. I couldn't sleep because my mind was racing. Finally I was in the city, snug in my little shoebox apartment—my own tiny slice of real estate in the most amazing city in the world. No, I didn't have a job yet, but that was just a matter of time. I had found my city and surely it wouldn't take more than a moment or two for it to take me in its arms and let me sample all that it had to offer.

I would go to galleries and museums, shop at Barney's, drink espresso at outdoor cafés, sprinkle my words with Italian phrases, ride the subway with the *Times* tucked under my arm. Gradually but assuredly, fabulous new alliances and opportunities would come my way. I would collect exotic, cultured friends who would welcome me into their fold. Inevitably, I would date a string of handsome, exciting men— all with some new talent or attribute—Marco the actor, Bartholomew the cellist, Gustavo the linguist. My life would become a series of glamorous and impossibly cool vignettes in which I starred, of course. I would be the girl in black smoking a Silk Cut, tossing her Philip Treacy hat in the air as a gaggle of midwestern tourists looked on, both mystified and intrigued.

That next morning after my arrival, my first day as a New Yorker, I trudged out into the snow, which had piled up to more than a foot overnight, immobilizing the city and emptying the streets of its usual chaos. I walked and walked and walked that day—downtown to Battery Park City, up through Chinatown and then west to SoHo, north a few blocks and over to the Hudson, up and up and up to Riverside Drive and then east through Central Park. By the time I reached the other side, dusk had fallen. I walked down Fifth Avenue with wide eyes taking in the grandly sculptured buildings, the stoic and starched doormen, complete with tan felt top hats and white gloves.

I was outside, of course, but I felt like I was walking through a posh and vaulted parlor. The street was empty, save a few chauffeurs standing next to idling, sleek black cars with smoky windows and gleaming exteriors. I felt as if I'd come upon the missing piece of the city's jumbled puzzle. It seemed as if the whole mania and excess of New York's collective life could be traced back to this street, this quiet pocket of calm tranquility, opulence and ease. This tiny stretch of land on this tiny sliver of an island was the prize, the goal, the inner sanctum. This was Oz.

I imagined walking through one of these grand entrances, riding the smooth elevator up and up and up to the very top apartment. I saw myself out on the terrace looking at my unobstructed, above-the-trees view of Central Park. And I exhaled.

That night, I sat alone at the counter of Veselka, pretending to read a *Village Voice* (but really just spying on the people around me) while sipping a…

"Coffee?"

"What?" I said, jolted out of my reverie.

"Would you like some coffee?" Svetlana leaned over the table now, her right hand poised to pour coffee into my empty mug, her coral-stained lips stretched into a kind smile.

"Yes, she definitely needs coffee." I heard a voice from behind me.

It was Tess.

She leaned over to kiss my cheek. Her hair fell long and loose, which she rarely let it do and her cheeks were flushed from the cold. She seemed radiant with energy.

"Lena, what's going on? I raced over here."

"I'm okay," I said, not even convincing myself.

"I don't think you are."

I paused, suddenly realizing how much I didn't want to go into the gory details of the past hour of my life.

"Honey, what is it?"

"I am such a fool," I said finally. "He's been cheating on me with Cecily this whole time."

"What? You're not serious?" Tess seemed truly shocked. "Tell me what happened."

And so I did—in one long, painful monologue, interrupted only by hiccups, nose blowing, and an occasional moment of silence as I searched in vain for the appropriate descriptive terms to clearly convey the awfulness of the past day and the pathetic hopelessness of my present.

"You were right, Tess. You've been right all along," I said.

"Right about what?" Tess's voice was soft.

"I've been living in a dream world. Men cannot be trusted. There were so many signs—I just refused to see them."

"You *did* see them, Lena. You just had the wrong girl."

"But I shouldn't have trusted him from the start, Tess. You

never would have thrown yourself into a relationship the way I did." I shook my head. "You told me over and over. And I just wouldn't listen…."

Tess clicked her tongue. "Would you stop blaming yourself?"

"I won't be mad if you feel like telling me 'I told you so,'" I said. In fact, I really wanted to hear Tess launch into one of her frequent diatribes against the universal sham of romantic love and the general uselessness of the male population. For some reason though, she wasn't taking the bait. And she *always* took the bait.

"Lena, don't say that. You're going to find the right guy, I promise. It'll all work out."

Huh? Tess? What the hell was she talking about?

"You're hurting right now—understandably. But it's going to get better, I promise," she said, patting my hand.

"Tess, that's so *optimistic* of you." I searched her face for clues. "What's going on?" I said, suspiciously.

"What do you mean?" She laughed and looked away.

Okay, something was definitely going on.

"Is there something you're not telling me, Tess?"

"Honey, let's just concentrate on you. You've had such a traumatic day and—"

"Come on. Humor me here."

She paused. "Well, it's not such a big deal."

"Go on."

"Okay." She looked down at her hands as she slowly formulated her confession. "I was at French Roast earlier, but it wasn't to have coffee."

"Okay…"

"I was meeting someone there…"

"Right…"

"To go…"

"Yes…"

"On a date." She spilled the words out quickly and I wasn't sure at first what she had said.

"Tess, honey. It's okay. Just because I've sworn off men doesn't mean you can't date." I still didn't get it. Why the secrecy? Why the *optimism* for God's sake? "Do you really like him?" I asked gently.

"Yeah," she answered quickly, but still seemed to be holding back.

"Have you seen him more than once?"

"Yeah, a couple of times." She blushed and held her hands to her face.

"Tess, just tell me. Who is it? What's going on?"

"It's…Macho Macchiato." She looked down.

Wow, I thought.

"Wow," I said.

Tess didn't answer, she just continued to stare at her hands.

"So, what's he like?"

Tess sat up straight in her seat, ready to talk. The shock of it was over.

"Well, he's just…" Her gaze turned upward and she smiled as she talked. "He's just so great. He's funny and he's sensitive and he's just so, so kind. His name is Marcel. And he's smart and interesting…and just so kind. Did I mention that already?"

"Yeah."

"Oh," Tess caught herself. "I'm sorry. I know it's not the time for all that. I guess I'm just excited." She looked at me sheepishly, not quite at ease with her giddiness but completely unable to tame it.

"Tess, stop it. I'm so happy for you. Really."

Tess looked at me with pained eyes. I knew she wanted me to be happy.

"And here you thought he was some nineteen-year-old out-of-work actor!" I tried to be upbeat.

"No," she smiled mischievously. "He's a twenty-one-year-old out-of-work dancer." She laughed.

"Where did you go for your date?"

"Oh, we haven't gone yet. I was just meeting him after his shift."

"What? Go on then, get out of here!"

"Are you kidding me? I'm not going anywhere."

"I'll be fine."

Tess stared at me, unconvinced.

"I'm serious. Go." I tried to summon a smile, but all I could muster was a lopsided smirk.

We sat like that for a moment—Tess mentally berating herself for admitting she had plans—not to mention, happy, romantic ones. I sat very still in the booth, using all my energy to portray a well-adjusted, mentally stable person.

"Okay, but I'm calling you tonight. No screening."

And then she left. I had wanted her to go. I didn't really want to spend my energy convincing her that I wasn't going to slit my wrists or maybe slit Colin's. Still I was surprised she left, and, selfishly, a little stung by it. But then again, hadn't I learned that men make you do crazy things? If I'd needed more conclusive proof—and I really didn't think I did at this point, thank you very much—a giddy Tess trotting off to meet her jailbait Joffrey dropout was certainly the clincher.

Alone again.

I dialed Parker's number, but I knew there was no chance of catching her free on a Saturday. I heard the first few words of her greeting and hung up.

I watched Svetlana line up glasses behind the counter while she talked on the phone. What was she saying? Something about her sister, or was it her mother? She would pick up the prescription, yes, and don't forget the roast was in the fridge. She seemed like the kind of woman who was always taking care of others. Family, friends, customers. She was the one who cleaned up the kitchen, shopped for the groceries, made dinner, wiped noses, cleaned drains, picked up clothes, poured coffee and folded laundry. And here she was smiling at me, pouring *me* coffee, comforting *me*.

She didn't wear a wedding ring. Never married? Maybe her no-good husband had left her for a younger Oksana. Maybe there hadn't been a husband at all. Whatever the case, I assumed she was alone now. The city was full of lifetime loners—mostly women and mostly not by choice. These were the odd women out who were left still standing when the music stopped. I'd see them pushing wire shopping carts, sitting alone in coffee shops, waiting for the bus— going about their lives in a city that saw them as an afterthought if they thought about them at all. No matter how happy or successful they may be, they were viewed with a certain suspicion and, much worse, a heavy dose of pity. Love was as cut-throat and competitive as everything else here. Good men were more rare than a rent-stabilized one-bedroom with a view.

I got up from the table and took a seat on one of the bar stools, the very same spot where I had sat on that first snowy night. It was also the night I met Jake.

"Mind if I read part of your paper?" he had said in what I later realized was just a lame attempt to start a conversation. He took the seat next to mine.

"Take the whole thing," I had answered, without even glancing his way. There was too much human drama going on around me to bother with a paper, I remembered thinking. At that particular moment, I was transfixed by a young couple arguing in the corner. The woman wore a fleece-lined jean jacket and red leather pants, the man wore a fuzzy aviator hat that he kept on even while he ate. At first they had tried to be quiet, but now things were too heated for them to care. I could just barely hear what they were saying. He was upset—he never saw her, she was spending too much time with her friends, too many hours at work—he felt neglected. She was sorry—but couldn't give up her independence—he kept trying to change her. Why did he want her to be someone else, she wanted to know. Why did he want to stifle her?

"She is so pathetic." I heard a voice from behind me.

"I'm sorry?" I had said, a little confused as I turned to see Jake for the first time. (I was still polite in those days.)

"Look at her. She's so self-righteous."

"How can you say that?" I said, agitated.

He smiled now. He had my attention.

"It's all about body language. She's clearly lying to him."

I had looked at Jake, closer this time. He was very attractive—this I noticed right away, but there was something else, too. Something about him made me want to talk to him, to know him.

"But she's practically crying," I said, still perplexed.

"Mmm, no. I'm sorry." He had examined them with the clinical eye of a scientist. "This is going to break wide open any second."

I paused. "You're awfully sure of yourself, aren't you?"

"I'm sure of some things, yeah." And then he gave me my first ever "Jake look"—a cocky half smile, accompanied by an intense gaze. Very intense. At that moment, I sensed a commotion behind us, aviator man was accusing red leather woman that she was cheating on him. She was angry but she wasn't denying it. Her face looked different now, harder. She was telling him that maybe she wouldn't have to cheat if he could satisfy her once in a while. I was beginning to lose my sympathy for her.

I had turned to Jake in awe. He sipped from his latte, unmoved.

"You're amazing," I said.

"I know," he agreed.

It wasn't until several months later that I discovered Jake himself had been helping red leather woman two-time her man.

And I didn't realize that Jake had been hitting on me for a few months longer than that. But by that time I knew his game or at least I thought I did. In his revolving alliances, I had managed to secure a steady lead role. From the very beginning, we talked at least twice a day about anything and everything—my strange encounter at the dry cleaner, his annoyance with incompetent Starbucks employees, our mutual dislike of cold days that are sunny, why blue and yellow make green.

But I couldn't talk to him now. I picked up my phone, flirting with the temptation of calling him. Just the idea that I could press one button on my speed dial and hear his voice made me feel better. But what would I say?

I needed to see him. I felt the energy welling up inside me. I would just tell him—you were right and I was wrong. He had tried to warn me about Colin and I wouldn't listen. I need you, I would say. I'm sorry, I would say. It was so clear to me now, so simple. I hopped off the bar stool, plunked down a twenty-dollar bill for Svetlana, grabbed my coat and was off. I felt like a kid running down the stairs to the Christmas tree, the anticipation was so intoxicating. I ran/walked down the streets to the Lower East Side. I passed a candy store and doubled back, securing a hefty bag of

Swedish fish—his favorite (a little candy bribe couldn't hurt!) As I made my way, my fears began to disintegrate even further. I would apologize—I *should* apologize. I'd been so careless, I now realized. I'd just forgotten all about Jake in my stupid Colin haze. Jake and I had a rule—friends first, sex second. I had broken the rule! A simple clarity was emerging.

I waved to Randolph, the homeless man who took up temporary residence on the heating grate outside Jake's building and ran inside. I stomped up the six flights of stairs until I reached his door. Catching my breath, I tried to remember the words that I had planned to say.

I miss you, Jake. I'm sorry. I've been so distracted lately. I... couldn't remember the rest. It didn't matter, I wouldn't have to get that far I was sure of it. I knocked and waited. No answer. I knocked again, nothing. No, he had to be there— I couldn't take the anticipation much longer. I could hear music from inside. He must be there—maybe he just couldn't hear over the stereo. I knocked again. My knuckles were beginning to ache and I was forced to consider the possibility that he might not be home.

"Dammit," I said, more sad than mad.

And then the door swung open as if those were the magic words.

"Vanessa?" My voice (and my stomach) fell flat.

"Nora?" She mocked my surprise. I didn't correct her. It suddenly seemed plausible that perhaps I had wandered into the wrong building. I was quite stressed-out, after all.

"May I help you?" she said, in the most unhelpful tone possible. She leaned comfortably against the door frame, one hand extended out, resting on the doorknob like a barricade. She wasn't wearing shoes. My God, what had happened since I last talked to Jake? I felt like Rip van Winkle.

"What are you doing here?" There really wasn't much reason to feign friendliness.

"Visiting Jake." She smiled, fully cognizant of the indirectness of her first direct answer.

"Is he here?"

She paused for a moment as if she had to think. Please— the apartment wasn't that big.

"No," she finally decided.

"Is he coming back anytime soon?"

"Later," she answered, conveying nothing except for the very clear message that she was done with our chat.

"Ooh, are those Swedish fish?" She looked down at my pathetic bag of candy.

"How cute." She cocked her head in a way that indicated the very opposite, that the sight of a twenty-seven-year-old woman carrying a bag of rainbow-colored candy was, well, pathetic.

"I'll be sure to tell Jake you stopped by," she said, and closed the door firmly.

And that's when the tears began yet again. I sprinted down the stairs, streaming a school of Swedish fish along the way.

chapter 12

I wasn't exactly startled when I noticed Super Si standing in my bedroom. I think my senses were too numb at that point to register the event as anything more than mildly unusual.

"Si." I smiled but made no motion to get up. I was pleased, or something close to it. A friendly face at last.

"Hello, Lena, glad to see you're okay," he said kindly.

I couldn't commit to an answer so I just smiled a non-committal smile. And then I heard the unmistakable, frenetic tap of Parker's shoes (her brown suede Gucci stilettos with leather piping if I wasn't mistaken) making their way across my linoleum kitchen floor.

"Lena?" Her voice was frantic. She entered the room, swathed in pashmina, her hair neatly contained in a tight, low ponytail, her vintage Kelly bag held close to her side. She was in work mode.

"Thank God, you're all right." Her voice took the angry, irritated tone of a mother who, upon realizing that her child is in fact alive and well, finds her grief has turned to gall.

"Parker?"

"Thank God I got here when I did."

What would have happened if she hadn't, I pondered?

"And I had to track down Si…thank you so much for this, Si."

"No problem. I'll leave you two alone." Si winked at me. He understood.

"Okay, Lena, get up. You need to get out of that bed. Pronto."

"Parker, I'm fine."

She looked at me with exaggerated disbelief.

"What? I'm fine," I said, tears rolling down my face.

"Oh really?"

Then I had a thought.

"How do you even know what happened?

"Uh, you called me."

"But I didn't leave a message."

"I know—which you know is a pet peeve of mine." She raised her voice. "But we'll save that for another time."

"So, how did you—?"

"Hello? Caller ID?" She looked exasperated. "And then I had to get the full report from Tess—who sounded totally bizarre herself. What is going on with all of my friends, for God's sake?"

I turned over on my bed, my back facing Parker. She sighed loudly.

"Get up."

"I'm not getting up." Didn't she have an assistant to torture?

"Lena, I'm not leaving here until you are out of that bed."

My heart stood still. I could feel the bed shift as she sat down next to me.

"You're distressing me, Lena. It's not like you to be this…sedentary."

I thought for a moment. "Sure it is."

My mind clicked into gear. Strategy #1: Lie.

"Parker, I've totally been up today. I'm just taking a nap, that's all. I've got like a whole *list* of things to do today."

"Really. Like what?"

I cringed. "What day is it again?"

"Oh, my God! Lena!"

"What?" I complained, pulling the covers over my head. She ripped them back away from me. "Lena!" She sounded horrified. She was looking at my bare legs.

"What?" I was horrified by her horror. I sat up.

"When were you planning on shaving your legs?"

"The next time I plan to have sex," I said dryly. "Likely never." I swung my legs over the side of the bed.

"With that attitude you won't." She sat down next to me. "I think I know what you need."

"You do?" I raised one brow, curious.

"Yes." Her eyes lit up. Parker was in pitch mode. She fumbled around with her bag, finally brandishing a crisp white business card as if it were a fine jewel.

"I'm positive that Sheila can help you." Parker handed me the card, which was engraved with the following words: "Sheila Sunshine, Life Coach."

"A life coach?" The words came out of my mouth with a reflexive laugh.

"She's amazing." Parker's voice was solemn. "She can help you."

"A therapist, Parker? Come on. I've been to therapy. I'm *impervious* to therapy. It's a fact."

"She's not a therapist. It's not about those silly 'I wasn't breastfed, therefore I'm not complete' crap. It's about your *future,* not your past."

"Parker…" I hesitated. "Did you go to see Sheila?" I treaded softly here.

Parker straightened her shoulders, hesitating. "Maybe one or two sessions." And then she added, "It's not just me. Penelope Cruz and Stella McCartney *swear* by her."

"Look, Parker, I'm sure she's very…talented. It's just not for me, that's all." I handed back the card.

Strategy #2: Deceive.

I was already upright, my legs dangling on the floor. I may as well get up and pretend to be "active." That way, Parker could get back to work and I could get back to wallowing.

"You know what? I'm actually feeling a lot better." I stretched my arms and got up.

"You are?" Parker eyed me suspiciously.

"Yeah." I forced a smile. "I think I'll go to the gym, in fact." I went to the bathroom, pretending to make noise. I shoved on my running shoes and wrapped my coat over my pajamas.

"Ready?" I came out of the bathroom. I'd walk her to the corner, take a detour at the deli (I really needed some more Hostess cupcakes, anyway) and then double back.

Parker didn't budge.

"Lena, open your coat."

"Why?" I tried to look mystified.

"Because."

"No, I'm cold."

Parker lunged for me, grabbing my coat. I made a quick turn to pull away, but it was too late.

"Lena!"

"What?" I flung myself onto the bed. "How many times are you going to say my name like that? I already feel badly enough."

Parker didn't answer. I felt her sit down on the edge of the bed and then lie down beside me, our backs facing each other.

"Lena. I'm not leaving here."

And I knew she meant it.

Strategy #3: Accept Defeat.

"I'm glad our paths have found a way to cross today."

Sheila Sunshine looked at me meaningfully from the other side of her tidy desk. She wore dark tortoiseshell frames that had the shape of cat's eyes. Her hair was a curly mop that seemed to sit on her head as opposed to being attached to it. She was smiling and had been since I'd walked into her tiny incense-filled office not ten minutes ago. I wished she would stop.

"Okay, today is our first session of what will, I know, be a transforming and revelatory experience for both of us," she said, smiling even more brightly. "That's right," she said, as if my impassive face had somehow conveyed an expression to her.

"You see, Lena—I consider this to be a mutually beneficial relationship. We learn from each other." More smiling. "Today's our first day together and I want to introduce you to some of the broader themes of my system." She reached into the top drawer of her desk and pulled out a stack of brightly hued flash cards.

"Now, I'm just going to scroll through these cards and let their message sink into your brain." Her voice had dropped down to a husky whisper now. "Don't say a word—just let the ideas flow into your consciousness." She lit a candle, dimmed the lights and we were off. Slowly she scrolled through the cards, each one offering a different instructive verb.

"Relax."

"Reevaluate."

"Reinvigorate."

"Renew."

"Replenish."

"Reignite."

I did feel relaxed—and had been since I'd entered the room, which may have explained why I hadn't bolted the second she switched on the Yanni CD. Maybe I was just too tired to move.

I looked back at Sheila. Still smiling. What must it be like to have convinced yourself so firmly that you had found the "way," so much so that you felt compelled to offer your services to others, convinced that their problems would quickly evaporate once you'd given your prescription for happiness.

Sheila's eyes had closed now. I noticed the patch of bleached hair over her top lip, her small, childlike hands with paint-chipped nails, rotating the flash cards. Suddenly I imagined Sheila in an entirely different life altogether—as a medical secretary or an airline ticket agent. She didn't seem to be fully comfortable with the life she led as Sheila Sunshine—sort of like a PTA Mom at a Hare Krishna retreat. I wondered what had made her choose this life, this job…that tunic. When had it become clear to her that she should paint her office walls purple and recite affirmations to total strangers? I could imagine her as an anonymous middle manager, trolling to the office each day in the same Liz Claiborne navy-blue suit and sensible Easy Spirit pumps, selling ad time for the local TV station or working in the employees-benefit department of a company that sold administrative software. I could see her vividly warming up a

Lean Cuisine frozen dinner of Fettucine with Herbed Chicken for lunch while stealing sugar and mustard packets in the staff kitchen. I saw her with friends named Lois and Linda, power-walking in matching sweatshirts on the weekend and then stopping for Dunkin' Donut munchkins on the way home. I did *not* see her living on an ashram in India, performing a downward facing dog, or eating a dragon bowl at Angelika's Kitchen.

Suddenly the lights were on and the music was off.

"I see you were really in a spell there. That's wonderful." Sheila was smiling (of course), but she did seem truly elated.

"Now I've got some homework for you to do." She handed me a thick file folder.

"All the instructions are inside," she assured me. "And I want you to hang these adhesives at different points in your living space," she added, handing me a stack of inscribed stickers. The one on top read: "The future is a swimming pool. Dive in!"

We stared at each other for a second. I decided it was my chance to speak.

"Sheila?"

"Yes?" She looked surprised (but still pleased!) to hear me speak.

"I was just wondering how you got into this line of work." Her smile quickly disintegrated. Whoops.

"Lena. We focus on the future here. Not the past. It's not important what we *were*—it's important what we'll *become*."

There would be no follow-up questions. We sat like that for a moment—I presumed until she felt the gravity of her words had sunk in adequately. Then, her hands together, she handed me my "homework packet" and stood up from her desk. The smile was firmly back in place.

I made my way to the door, feeling somewhat dazed

when she said: "Lena, you will find what you're looking for." Despite myself (and much to my embarrassment), the words gave me goose bumps.

In the hallway, as I waited for the elevator, I noticed a stack of mail. "To Sheila Rosenberg or current resident." Sheila Rosenberg?

Bing. The elevator doors opened.

The main concern preoccupying me as I sat waiting for Tess and Parker at the café at Bergdorf's was how to hide my legs from the liquid ladies (as in their cash flow and their lunches) dining (or pretending to) around me. You see I had been prodded by an old woman's umbrella as she forced the doors open on the number 6 train. Her aged aggression had left a ragged laceration down the side of my fishnets which, in this crowd, was tantamount to donning a scarlet A on one's cashmere Michael Kors twin set. Actually, I take that back—a badge of adultery probably wouldn't raise too many overplucked eyebrows in this place, as long as it was embroidered impeccably of, course.

"Hey, Lena…omigod, do you realize that you have the most hideous run down the side of your fishnets?" Parker had arrived.

"I know. Keep your voice down! Everyone will notice now."

"For God's sake—do you realize where we are?"

Parker may not be very religious, but she did hold some things sacred.

"Forgive me almighty Bergdorf for I have sinned."

"Can't you just go buy another pair and change in the bathroom?"

"Hose cost fifty dollars here!"

Parker looked at me blankly.

"Hey, guys, sorry I'm late." Tess breezed in, wearing jeans and a beautiful pale yellow peasant blouse; her hair hung in loose waves.

"Are you wearing jeans?" Parker shifted her attention from me to Tess. Tess never wore jeans.

"Stop it, Parker! You look fabulous, Tess." And of course she did. It was even more depressing to see her in an outfit that I could actually afford to wear, because I could no longer fool myself into thinking that she always looked beautiful because of her exquisite clothes. "I love that shirt."

"Thanks, I bought it on the street." Tess beamed with delight.

Parker inhaled. "For God's sake. Keep your voice down!" She looked exasperated. "What is wrong with you two today?"

"I'm starving. Let's order," I said, ignoring Parker as I opened the menu. I quickly shut it again.

"What's wrong, Lena?" Tess looked concerned.

"Oh, I guess I'm just not craving an eighteen-dollar salad for some reason," I said.

"Oh honey, I'll pay for it," Tess offered.

"No, absolutely not," I said firmly.

"What about a sixteen-dollar grilled-vegetable plate?" Parker offered ever so helpfully.

"No really. I'm fine."

"Listen, I'm buying you a six-dollar scone. No buts," Tess said with finality.

"She can't eat that scone! Are you crazy? These dresses don't have a millimeter of wiggle room," Parker said.

The dresses. Tess and I had spent months participating in an elaborate charade of Parker's design. She had encouraged us to snip out pictures we liked, held countless quorums on color and cut, and spent entire weekends presiding over grueling try-on sessions. We had weighed in with our opinions—black yes, lilac no; simple sheath yes, shoulder straps no. Parker had tried—she really had—to include us, please us, and not to bankrupt us. But when Dot the wedding planner had called with the news that three bridesmaids dresses identical to those chosen by Marie Chantal for her storybook wedding to Crown Prince Pavlos had been delivered to Bergdorf's, well, all hope was lost. The dresses were chosen. It was the way things should be. So that was the way things would be.

"Lena, how are things with Sheila?"

"Who's Sheila?" Tess asked.

"You really don't want to know," I answered.

"So?" Parker ignored my sarcasm. She wanted details.

"It was fine. Love that tunic of hers."

"Yeah, that is pretty dreadful, isn't it," Parker said, making a face. There was nothing like the reminder of a bad fashion choice to throw Parker off the scent. "That's not the point though—how *was* it?"

I paused. I didn't want to think about Sheila and all the sad drama that had brought me to her sad purple office.

"Will someone tell me who Sheila is?" Tess was perplexed.

"Lena's life coach," Parker said.

"You have a life coach?" Tess asked innocently.

"It's more like a therapist," I said.

"It is nothing like a therapist. Sheila helps people reengage with their lives," Parker snapped, and then quickly retained her composure. "Tess, speaking of reengaging with life. What's going on with you and this whole casual vibe?"

"What do you mean? Nothing's going on," Tess answered, so self-conscious that one couldn't help but assume something was definitely going on.

"What do you mean, 'what do you mean?' The jeans!"

Parker could not let go of the jeans.

"Well, I am very engaged with life right now, I would say." She smiled dreamily.

"Are you talking about your latte-lord-a-leaping? Lena mentioned him. That was an unexpected move," Parker said with one brow raised.

"But a good one," I quickly rejoined.

"It's just a fling, really," Tess demurred.

"Of course it is," Parker said, perhaps a bit too quickly for Tess's liking.

Awkward silence.

"So, here's three dollars," I said. "Anyone want to split a scone? That's a dollar a bite."

The Internet is an amazing invention. Staring at the blank box of a search engine, fully intending to begin your job search in earnest, it's virtually impossible not to be gripped by the compulsion to enter your name, your friend's name, a relative's name, a sworn enemy's name, or even a group of nonsensical letters.

Out of nowhere, I suddenly found myself typing Nadine's name. Wasn't she how I ended up in this mess in the first place? I couldn't believe that I hadn't thought to do a background check on her before. I mentally scolded myself as I greedily waited for the Google gods to deliver to me the dirt on Nadine's past. Just where had Satan's spawn honed her witchcraft? I waited, hungrily…and then it was revealed: A nonprofit film cooperative producing documentaries on social issues? Huh? There was even a quote attributed to her in an old *New York Times* story entitled "Filmmakers Making A Difference." She said, "Changing people's lives with your work is a greater reward than anything Hollywood has to offer." What? *Nadine?* How had this idealistic young woman morphed into the haggard, power-hungry, morally challenged person that she was today?

I was shocked, confused, and totally fascinated. And I was hooked.

I looked down at my desk and caught a glimpse of Sheila Sunshine's card. Let's just see exactly who Ms. Sheila Rosenberg really is, I thought, as I typed in her name and excitedly waited for my wish list of secret information to appear before me. I quickly narrowed down the selection to those in the tri-state area.

She had run a manicure salon! In suburban New Jersey, of course. She had two kids, was divorced, and ran the Montclair Thanksgiving Day 5K race. It was beginning to be clear to me why Sheila Sunshine wanted my attention on the future, not the past.

I typed my own name.

Lena Sharpe.

Three references to *Face to Face* appeared along with a link to my college alumni page, and several mentions of an altogether different Lena Sharpe who appeared to be a competitive high-school swimmer with a keen interest in ceramics, who had recently made an unsuccessful run for president of the Young Democrats Club. Lena Sharpe just can't get a break, I thought, pitying our collective disappointments.

And then, quickly and covertly, I typed *his* name. It was inevitable, I reasoned. I might as well get it over with. My heart hurt as I saw the reality of his name staring back at me on the screen. Immediately I set to work, my pulse racing as I quickly clicked on each entry. All of them appeared to be his—there seemed to be one and only one Colin Bates. With just a few clicks of the mouse, I uncovered new strands of information—he had played lacrosse, ran for student council president (and won), was a Fulbright scholar, and attended the wedding of Ryan and Christine Maythorpe. There were also the mentions of his book, several reviews as well as a few brief profiles. Several of his poems were listed on smug literary journal Web sites with knowingly silly names like "Rhyme Time." Further evidence of his emotional shallowness, I thought. This was disappointing—I had almost reached the end of the list. I didn't know what I had expected to find, but I certainly didn't feel any better. The Internet version of Colin Bates seemed to be just as overachieving and inscrutable as the real one. The last entry caught my eye and I clicked on it. It was from a Web site called "Juxta-prose" and read:

> "Simple Girl"
> *Her name is Lena. A simple girl. Uncluttered by knowledge, she moves through the world quietly, unnoticed. Her bright eyes grow brighter at the lights of the city, the thrill of its energy, its rhythms delight her, though she knows not why. Her pleasure is pure, her wonder immeasurable. She looks at me, her devotion unwavering, unquestioning. Her future a blank page, she eagerly hands me a pen and begs of me to write it for her.*

My first thought was *What a truly awful piece of writing*. My second thought was *I am the dumbest person on this planet*. How could I fall for such a complete jerk? There could be no rationalization now, no way to speculate that maybe— on some level—he loved me. I didn't know Colin Bates and it appeared I never had. That safety net had vanished and I felt like an alcoholic on her first day toward sobriety. I sat down on my bed, hugging my knees, letting the tears spill down my bended legs. I couldn't believe that I felt worse than before, that it was possible to feel worse than before.

★ ★ ★

The next few days were a blur of sleeping, listening to sad CDs and aimless, lonely walks. I had just gotten back from a matinee of *Love Story* at the revival movie theater on my corner when I noticed a note from Parker stuck to my door with an adhesive that was imprinted with, "*Your soul has something to say. Are you listening?*—From the office of Sheila Sunshine."

The note from Parker read:

"I was in your hood for a meeting. Glad to see that you're out and about! Call me—I need to talk to you for a sec."

I picked up my cell phone and a nail file. I called Parker while I set about chipping off Sheila's pseudo-spirit-lifting nonsense. She picked up on the first ring.

"Hey, Parker. Sorry I missed you. I was out at an…interview."

"Oh, that's *great*. What was it for?"

"Oh, you know, it was at a company that makes…nail files."

"Oh, I see."

"Yes, it's a multinational conglomerate specializing in the cosmetic industry." I was trying to bullshit The Bullshitter. I had better shut up and fast.

"Well, that sounds great," she said encouragingly.

That sounds great? That was weird. She just totally let that slide. Parker didn't let anything slide.

"You're coming to taste cakes with me and Tess this Saturday, right? Don't forget."

"Of course." Now I was suspicious. "Anything else you wanted to tell me?" I asked.

"Well, it's about Sheila."

"Oh yes, I got the lovely adhesive on my door. Thanks so much."

"But it's a really beautiful sentiment, don't you think?"

"Well, yes—and it better be, because I'm having a lot of difficulty scraping it off my door." I dug the nail file in more deeply.

"Well, anyway…what I wanted to tell you is that Sheila might—"

At that moment I heard my landline ring.

"One sec, Parker…hello?"

"Lena, dear?"

Sheila Sunshine.

"You gave her my number, Parker?" I put the cell phone to my other ear.

"Lena, you need to talk to someone," Parker said.

"Would you *please* leave me alone?" I begged.

"Which one of us are you talking to?" Parker asked.

"Both of you."

"Just talk to her," Parker pleaded.

"Lena, could you just talk to me?" Sheila pleaded.

"Honestly, both of you. Can't you just let me mope in peace?"

Parker: "Give her ten minutes."

Sheila: "Give me ten minutes."

"Parker, I'm hanging up on you. I will see you at the tasting." I closed my cell phone. "Sheila, you have one minute and then you have to promise that our paths will never cross again. Deal?"

"Okay, that's fine," she said reluctantly. Thank God, I thought. I wondered if she was this pushy with all her clients.

I slunk down in a chair at the kitchen table and set about examining the nutritional information for a box of Lucky Charms.

"Lena, I'm concerned," Sheila began.

"Really."

"Your behavior is troubling and toxic."

"Is that so?"

"Lena, why did you want Colin to love you? Or better yet, why do you think Colin was able to deceive you?"

"It's hard to say."

"Weren't there ever times when you questioned his motives, his intent?"

I didn't respond. I sat very still, but I felt my hands start to quiver a little.

"Lena, what do you want for yourself?"

"Sheila, why don't *you* tell me what I want? All I'm hearing are questions," I challenged her. "You know, never mind, I have to go now." I hung up the phone before she could answer.

My phone rang again almost immediately after I placed it on the handset.

"Jesus, Sheila. This has to stop," I answered.

"Lena?"

I immediately tensed. It wasn't Sheila.

"Lena, it's Chase." He had me on speaker.

"Cheese?" New rule: Do not answer the phone.

"Did you just call me Cheese?" He picked up the receiver. "Did *you* start that?"

"What do you want?"

"You know, all the interns keep asking if I'm Swiss…" I could almost hear the pieces clicking together in his head.

"I'm hanging up in three seconds."

"Do you know where Colin is?" he asked.

"What? Why?" Now he had my attention.

"Because I've tried him at home and I can't find his cell number."

"No, I mean—why do you want to talk with Colin?"

"We're supposed to have dinner tonight, but I need to reschedule."

"You've been speaking with Colin?"

"That's right. Quite a bit, actually." I'm sure he must have been enjoying my confusion, but I was too stunned to cover myself.

"Yeah, Nadine's thinking about having him come on the show as a part-time correspondent."

"Oh please! He would never do that…" But then I caught myself. Of course Colin would do something like that. Why could I not accept the fact that Colin was not the person I thought he was?

"Really? Because it was his idea. I'm just so surprised he hasn't shared any of this with you, Lena. You two seemed so…close," he said.

I caught my breath and hung up the phone.

I lay down on my bed and closed my eyes tightly until all I could see were psychedelic swirls. And then, without thinking, the image of Colin's frantic eyes, begging for my questions at the sit-down interview, popped into my head, refusing to be ignored. I had pushed that moment aside, just like I had the evening at Vanessa's when he had paid as much attention to me as he did the coasters on the coffee table. Then there were those late nights with Knox. My eyes were still shut, but suddenly I saw things more clearly. Why had I been so blind before?

A few hours later, I forced myself to leave my apartment. A winter chill had crept into the air and I pulled my coat tight around me. I trudged down Houston watching my feet take each step, with no idea where they were headed. I wondered vaguely when I would know it was time to go home.

When I saw the glowing red sign as I glanced down Essex Street, however, I immediately found myself walking toward it. Part of it had burned out and I couldn't read what it said, but it kept pulling me forward.

Finally I was upon it. "B-A-R" it read.

I pushed the heavy wooden door open and walked inside. It was dark and the air was thick and moist. It felt safe. I gravitated toward a corner booth next to the bar and the vinyl cushion crunched as I sat down. Someone had etched "Jason & Crystal 4-ever" into the table. I wondered where Jason and Crystal were right that moment. Did they come back to this table every so often to visit their names and toast their everlasting love? Did they still feel the kind of passion that inspired the defacement of property? Or were they long separated, flung out in different parts of the world, each scratching out their new unions on new bar tables as if for the first time?

I looked around the nearly empty room. In one corner an elderly man sat alone in a chair next to the jukebox, resting his hands on a cane. At the end of the bar, two younger men sat on bar stools side by side, each staring silently at their respective beer bottles, motionless.

This is the place where loneliness lived, I thought. The air felt crowded with daydreams. Lost loves, missed connections, moments of happiness, and even more moments of regret. At night, the tenor would change, of course. The space would swell with people and a desperate, hungry searching would take over, with bodies jostling for space and attention, forcing connections, drowning inhibitions. Still, the loneliness would be there, lurking just under the aimless chatter and drunken shuffle.

A bartender with greasy gray hair gathered in a loose ponytail approached my table and wiped it down with a dirt-streaked towel.

"What'll it be?" he asked gruffly, without a glance at me.

"Uh, a Scotch and soda, please," I said timidly.

He looked satisfied with my answer. This was no place to order a pink drink.

"I'll have the Scotch. She'll just have the soda," an unseen voice countered. The bartender and I both turned to see Si, newly arrived, his cheeks red from the cold.

"Hey, Si, coming right up." The bartender made his way back to the bar.

"Didn't expect to see you down here," Si said as he took off his non-ironic trucker's hat. It was odd seeing him outside of my building. I felt nervous, but I wasn't exactly sure why.

"I didn't really expect to be here myself," I said quietly.

"This place has a way of luring you in," he said more to himself than to me.

"There you go, buddy." The bartender made a clicking noise with his tongue.

Si grabbed our drinks from the bar and slipped into the seat across from me.

He took a slow sip of Scotch. We sat in silence for a while, long enough so that the peculiarity of sitting in a window booth of a dingy bar in the middle of a Wednesday afternoon with my sixty-something super began to dissipate somewhat. My thoughts drifted past my present pain and I wondered what had brought Si here. I pictured him as existing only in my building—stupid, I know—as natural and necessary as the front door and the fire escape. He lived alone, that much I knew. And he seemed lonely—lonely in a quiet way that seemed to indicate he was prepared to be that way for a long time. He belonged in this place.

"Do you come here a lot?" I asked.

"Most days," he said with a dry laugh. "Old friends around here," he muttered, glancing around the bar. "But you shouldn't. You've got too much in front of you to start looking backward."

"That's all I ever seem to do these days," I said, and tried to think of something else we could talk about. Caulking, perhaps? More silence. I reached for his Scotch and poured half of it into my soda.

"A drink's only gonna make it worse, Lena," he said.

"Who says anything's wrong?" I said, maybe a little too quickly given the fact that he'd had to help Parker forcibly enter my apartment to check on me just a few days earlier.

"What's his name?" he said finally.

"Who?" I asked.

"You know who," he said, not missing a beat.

"Colin," I said flatly. It felt so odd to sum up all my problems in two syllables.

"I've seen him around, I believe," he said, in a not entirely approving way.

"Well, what did you think?" I was curious now. I was obviously not a good judge of people, but something told me Si would be. He took his time with an answer.

"My guess is…"

"Yes?" I said, anxiously.

"He's a firefly," he said decisively.

"A what?"

He put his drink down now. "You know how when you were a kid, you would chase fireflies all over the yard. And just as soon as you got near one, it would turn off its light and disappear?"

"Yeah…" I was beginning to wonder if Si had been to a few other bars before this one. "I mean, I guess."

"And then, every now and then you would catch one in your hands and you could see it up close?" These were the most words I think I had ever heard Si utter at one time.

"And then you realize when you're sitting there with this insect between your hands that that's all it is. An insect. Like an ordinary housefly. Or a mosquito," he said as if he had come to this realization a long time ago but was still amazed by it.

"But, I don't—"

He stopped me midsentence. "Stop chasing fireflies, Lena." He looked me in the eye. "Trust me on this one." Si folded his arms as if to indicate there would be no further discussion about it. I wanted to argue with him, but the more I turned the idea over in my head, the more it made a strange kind of sense.

Fireflies. My whole life had been full of them I now realized, swarming around me elusively, baiting me at every turn. In my mind's eye, everything was newer, better, more glamorous just around the corner. The next party, the next job, the next guy. The present was a waiting room, a holding pen, a moment *to be gotten through.* I had convinced myself that things were always about to change at any minute, and then my real life and my fantasy one would instantly meld into one.

"Lena, why did you want Colin to love you?" I could hear Sheila's voice in my head now.

Why did I want Colin to love me? Because I loved him. Or I had thought I did. Because he was handsome and smart and mysterious. Because he was a writer, living his life the way he wanted to live it, on his own terms. Because he was part of another world, a better world, the inner sanctum. He had the key to the apartment on the top floor of the beautiful building facing the park with the huge terrace and the white-gloved doorman, the one I had imagined on my first day in New York. And then I saw myself on the balcony, Colin's Easthampton balcony. My imagination had come to life.

And this is where it had led me.

Si picked up his Scotch and finished the last swirl. "Well, I better be going." He got up from the booth and pulled his hat down over his forehead.

"Si," I said, not looking up at him.

"Yes, ma'am."

"What's her name?"

"Who?"

"You know who." I looked him in the eye.

He paused for a second and I thought he might not answer.

"Shirley," he said finally. "Her name was Shirley." And with that, he patted my shoulder and turned to leave.

Soon enough, the heavy wooden door began to creak open more frequently, delivering a gasp of cold air and a sprinkling of nine-to-fivers with each motion; administrative assistants, systems analysts and marketing managers recently released from their workday obligations, ordering up colorful cocktails and jamming quarters in the glowing jukebox.

I sat there for a while thinking about Si and Shirley, Tess and Marcel, Parker and Brad, me and Colin, all these couples searching in the darkness, grasping at the air, like kids chasing…fireflies.

The next day, I had an idea. An irresistibly alluring idea. All I needed was an irresistibly alluring name with a fake e-mail account. I sat down at my computer and got to work. The name: Samantha Seabrook. The e-mail: *Sammygirl@hotmail.com*

Dear Mr. Bates:
I just read "Simple Girl" and I had to write. It's amazing. Your

description of this simple, naive girl is just so moving, so *evocative*. I'm in awe. If only my writing could be so inspired.
Yours,
Samantha

I felt better just having my deception out there, floating its menace throughout cyberspace. Samantha, my suitably seductive alter ego, was in charge now, and I had full faith that she was up to the task.

I was busy reading an e-mail from Parker about floral arrangements when I realized that I had already received a reply.

Samantha,
I am so touched by your kind words. You know what they say though—every great writer requires a great reader. Perhaps I've found one in you. Tell me, what sort of writing do you do?
—cb

I wanted to vomit. The gauzy veil of self-delusion had been successfully—and completely—lifted, that much was now painfully clear. How had I ever fallen for this guy? I could barely manage to type out the following words.

Mr. Bates,
Oh, I couldn't even begin to talk about my writing with you. I hardly get the time to devote to it that I'd like, what with my full-time modeling schedule. I must be content to learn by your example.
Samantha

Samantha,
Nonsense! I think it is my responsibility as a published author to encourage new voices. I'm pretty good about sens-

ing when an artist is serious about their craft and I have to
say, Samantha, I get that sense about you.
—cb
p.s. Tell me, what kind of modeling do you do? I dabble a
bit in photography myself....

I could not believe what I was reading. It had been so easy
to deceive him. How on earth did this moron manage to
fool *me* for so long, I wondered? I let a few days pass before
I responded. Finally I wrote to him.

Mr. Bates,
I'm so very sorry for the delay. I was away on a shoot in Mustique. Gisele got a nasty case of food poisoning and I ended
up having to do both the swimwear *and* the lingerie layouts.
But I'm sure this all seems so shallow to you! How I would
love to live the life of the mind like you do.
Samantha

Colin's response came within a matter of seconds. He was
so predictable, I sighed.

Samantha,
First of all, I insist that you call me Colin. I must tell you I spent
many of my boyhood summers in Mustique. Is it too much
to say that I can see you in my mind's eye, sunning yourself
on the beaches of the Caribbean?
—cb

Colin,
Oh, you're so very charming. I'm blushing terribly right now,
if only you could see me.
Samantha

Samantha,
I would love nothing more than to see you, in fact. Bring your writing and I'll give you a critique. When are you free?
—cb

I was physically ill. I deserved so much better than him. Hell, Cecily deserved so much better than him. For God's sake, even *Samantha* deserved better. It was almost enough to make me stop this charade entirely. Almost. I continued.

Colin,
I'm so moved by the generosity of your spirit, but remain much too timid for a face-to-face meeting. Maybe if I sent you a sample of my writing, you could decide if I'm worth your time....
Samantha

Sam—
With great haste, please send it to me.
—cb

I gathered myself together for the pièce de résistance.

"City Boy"
Pen poised, he sat at the grand, mahogany table, his framed degrees boldly announcing his esteemed pedigree on the wall behind him like a peacock's proud display of plumes. He *was* the peacock—the favorite son, the grand inheritor, the vessel of hope, the receiver of every privilege and luxury. He read the greats—Bellow and Roth, Fitzgerald and Faulkner, their first editions lined his shelves. Their spines gleamed in triumph, peering over his slumping shoulders, mocking his inertia and the limp wrist of his writing hand. He fancied himself the next Franzen and amused his audience with his

bravado as he ran his fingers through his brittle, thinning hair, his signet ring gleaming, his talent withering.

When I finished, I quickly highlighted Colin's e-mail along with the list of Juxta-prose contributors' e-mails, and, without a hint of reluctance, hit the "send to all" key and closed my computer. It would end as it began—in a flirtatious, misleading, altogether unfortunate e-mail exchange.

chapter 13

Of course I called Tess immediately to share the news.

"Oh my God, I can't believe you wrote that!" Tess giggled after hearing about my e-mail exchange with Colin.

"Yeah, it felt pretty liberating, I have to admit," I said. "I can't believe I never thought to Google him before."

"I know, that's such a necessary dating step these days. Although I think it can be detrimental."

"Why?"

"Well, because it rushes the natural evolution. You just shouldn't know too much about someone before you can *get* to know them."

"I see your point. Oh, and guess what else I found out?"

"What?"

"I looked up Nadine and it turns out she used to be a bleeding heart liberal!"

"What? I don't believe you," Tess said.

"I didn't believe it either at first, but it's true. She used to make documentaries about poverty and homelessness."

"Are you sure it's *your* Nadine?" She seemed skeptical.

"I'm positive. I guess you just never know about some people."

"Yeah, who would have thought she was actually…*interesting,*" Tess said. "I wonder how she became such a bitch."

"Maybe she met one too many Colins in her life," I said, wryly.

Tess was right, though. Nadine's life was a lot more intriguing than I had ever thought. I wasn't the same person that I was ten years ago—or even three months ago—so why did I assume that she had always been the person she was today? I had never really stopped to think about her life at all or the idea that her past could have been as circuitous and unpredictable as my own, full of disappointing relationships and lost idealism. And then I started to think about everyone else around me—the kindly superintendent, the sniveling co-worker, the New-Agey "life coach"—they were more than just bit players in my life's drama. They had lives of their own. They had stories of their own.

And then I had an idea.

Apparently, it was a cold day in hell on Tuesday morning. Because that was the morning that I negated every declaration I had previously made and once again crossed the threshold of Nadine Bollinger's corner office. This time, however, I had a mission. Today was the day for the black Armani suit.

As expected, Cheese was stationed out front at his lieutenant's position. As I approached, he was busy extricating his headset from the hanging plant it had somehow entangled itself in.

"Good morning, Chase."

"Well hello, I don't think we were expecting you today." He looked surprised, almost fearful. I was pleased. "What can we do for you?"

"You, Chase, can't do a thing for me I'm afraid. I do have a meeting with Nadine, however."

"I'm sorry, I'm just checking our schedule here, Nina."

"Lena."

"That's right, of course, Lena. And I don't believe we have any time for you just now, but if you'd like to re-schedule, I believe we might have something on, let's see—" he began flipping pages of the calendar rapidly, in-terminably "—March twenty-third."

"It's October, Chase."

"That's right. How's two-ish for you?"

"Sharpe." A disembodied voice barked my name. Nadine. I was almost nostalgic. Almost. "You can come in now."

I winked at Cheese and sailed past him.

"Close the door," Nadine instructed me once I was in-side her lair.

She looked the same, I noticed, except for what appeared to be the aftereffects of an unsuccessful session with a bot-tle of Sun-In.

"I was surprised to get your call, Sharpe. I don't usually keep up relationships with people I've fired."

"And to be honest, I didn't expect to find myself calling you, Nadine."

We stared at each other, waiting for the other to blink first.

"So, why did you agree to see me?" I said finally.

"I'm not sure. I was intrigued, I guess. I'm becoming less so each second we sit here. The clock's ticking. What's your pitch?"

I inhaled sharply and did my best to channel Parker. "You run a good show here, Nadine. It's slick, it's entertaining, it's well produced."

"Thanks, Sharpe, I'm so glad you approve."

"But it could be better…much better."

"Oh yeah, educate me." Nadine sat back in her chair, her arms crossed.

"Your show offers sixty minutes of celebrity worship. Pure and simple. In those sixty minutes, the viewer is treated to an inside view of the lives of the most privileged and pampered people in the world. We learn what toothpaste they use in the morning and how many stomach crunches they do in the evening. And do you know what that viewer is left with at the end of your show?"

"What?" Nadine asked dryly.

"A big, gaping, yawning void."

"So what are you saying, Sharpe?"

"I'm saying, Nadine, that your show—your viewers—are yearning for something more, something meaningful, something relevant to them and their lives. Your show, Nadine, is missing a heart."

"A heart?" Nadine guffawed loudly. "I don't give a rat's ass about giving this show 'heart.'"

"I think you do."

"Well, what the hell do you know?" She reached for her intercom. I was just an index finger away from being yanked out of her office by a vaudeville cane-wielding Cheese.

"I know about the documentaries."

She froze.

"I know you used to care about real people. I know it."

"Who have you been talking to?"

"This business has hardened you, but I know there's a heart down there somewhere. Isn't there, Nadine?" I moved in closer. "This show doesn't need another ten minutes devoted to celebrity grooming practices. It needs real people." I felt positively evangelical.

"What do you want, exactly?" she asked as if she were bargaining with a mugger.

"You need a correspondent. I need a job. I'll give you a ten-minute portrait each week profiling an average person, a real person, with the same exhaustive detail and loving care we give the celebs. It will work. And it will make this show better."

She was quiet for a moment and then she raised her head slowly. The two of us, eye to eye again.

"Okay, Sharpe," she said, but her voice had softened. I had her. "Keep talking."

chapter 14

"Sex with Tom Cruise," I said.

"When?"

I swallowed, deliberating for a moment.

"Definitely post *Top Gun*…but also pre *Mission Impossible*."

"Mmm…those were good years," Tess said with a smile.

The bakery assistant looked at us with bewilderment.

"I'm going to say *Jerry Maguire*," Parker chimed in.

"Wow. That might win it," I said, impressed.

Parker surveyed the scattered detritus of half-eaten cake slices around us. "Which one was like Richard Gere?"

"The chocolate mousse layer cake," I said.

"Okay, so we've got Tom, Mel post *Braveheart,* Richard Gere pre *Pretty Woman* and Marcel."

Parker and I looked at Tess. She shrugged, "I'm sorry. Movie stars just don't do it for me."

"God, I'm stuffed. I'm never going to be able to fit into

my dress for the engagement party," Parker said, stretching out her legs.

"Stop it, you're going to look gorgeous," Tess said.

"I'm just so stressed out. Do you have any idea how time consuming it is to plan a wedding?"

Tess and I exchanged a look.

"And Brad is no help at all. Somehow work always gets in the way."

"He's working hard for your money," I teased. Parker didn't smile. Next topic.

"So, Tess, how *is* Marcel?" I asked.

She smiled. "He's doing really well."

"I can't wait to meet him at the engagement party," Parker said.

"Oh, I'm not bringing him to the party." She looked startled by the idea.

"You're not?" Parker and I responded in unison.

"No, it's not like he's my boyfriend." She took another bite of cake, chewing with downcast eyes.

"He's not?" Parker and I asked at the same time again.

"No." She was clearly feeling uncomfortable.

Next topic.

"Lena, are you going to Jake's thing tonight?" Parker asked innocently.

"What thing?"

"His art opening," Parker said.

Jake. Art. Vanessa. Stairs. Swedish fish. I felt myself getting hot, the cloying sticky-sweet smell of confectionery sugar filled my lungs, my temples pounded.

"No, I doubt it," I said finally.

"Why not?" Again, another innocent Parker question.

"I wasn't invited."

Silence. Next topic.

"Tell me, which one was Mel Gibson?" The bakery assistant appeared, smiling, fork in hand.

I would go to see Jake that night. I had to. It was an important night for him. And no matter what had happened, we were friends—old friends, solid friends, maybe even best friends (if Jake were able to say the phrase without immediately asking to have a sleepover). I wasn't kidding myself, twisting reality, or manipulating the truth for my own purposes. Jake and I were friends that would last—not friends who fall away over time, reintroducing themselves every fifth year or so with a Christmas card, complete with pictures of unfamiliar children dressed in holiday colors, surrounded by wreaths and trees, or maybe a fuzzy puppy or two. No, we were face-to-face, phone-calls-daily, dinners-weekly, I-know-what's-in-your-fridge—and your medicine cabinet—where-you-bought-your-shoes, how-much-rent-you-pay friends. Period.

I was confident about this. And when I slipped into my new Nanette Lepore dress and slid into my Stephane Kelian pumps, I felt like a soldier preparing for battle. Vanessa be damned. She would, I felt at that moment, literally dissolve in my presence.

The scene was, predictably, a good one. On one brief half-block stretch, I encountered an Andy Warhol actor, Vincent Gallo, the current Calvin Klein men's underwear model and Lewis Lapham. I winked at Diego, who was tending the door, and made my way in. It was crowded, the air was thick with the vapors of status and money and lust. Jake had kept the lights low—even though this was an art showing—with only a single candle to illuminate each work. I ordered a vodka tonic and began to scan the crowd's perimeter.

It wasn't long before I caught sight of Vanessa holding

court in the center of the room. Most good parties (and Jake's were always good) had one particular person—almost always a woman—whose presence invigorated the room and sent a kind of electromagnetic charge throughout. She would be in the periphery of just about every man's line of vision (and not a few women's). She would be the sun around which all the other shifting constellations of party-goers would orbit.

Vanessa was definitely the sun tonight. She was the energy source, the power station, the fuel from which the party produced its energy. God, I hated her. Her skin was smooth and bronzed. Her dress was dramatic, what would be described in *Vogue's* fashion parlance as "deconstructed" with strangely shaped pieces of fabric strung together in what seemed to be only inconsequentially serving as coverage for the body. Vanessa, in that dress, became avant-garde, progressive and intrinsically cool. Most women would look like they were wearing a trash bag.

I started to make my way around the space—which, I noted, Jake had done an excellent job of keeping just raw enough. I surveyed the art—mostly paintings, with the few odd sculptural pieces thrown in for good measure. In the corner, a nude couple covered only in silver paint contorted themselves into various intertwining postures—collecting an audience of awed bankers' wives. It was a typical gallery show in which the act of viewing art was secondary to both the act of being seen viewing art as well as watching others view said art.

I hadn't gotten very far along when one particular painting caught my eye. It looked familiar. It looked like me. A voice came from behind me.

"No, you're not imagining it."

Jake.

I turned and smiled. I could feel my heart in my throat. "I'm so glad to see you," I said.

He didn't answer.

He looked so perfect in his black suit and three-day stubble. He seemed to be every bit the downtown curator that he meant to portray.

"Did you paint this, Jake?" Who else would have painted it? I thought. I was shocked and touched. It made me miss him more desperately than I already did. He said nothing.

"How've you been?" I asked tentatively.

"I've been okay."

Awkward silence had never been an issue for Jake and me. I felt that my very presence repulsed him.

"Listen, can we go outside for a second?" I asked.

"Why?"

"I just want to talk to you."

"We're talking."

I didn't say anything. I just looked at him stone-faced in front of me and wondered if Jake would ever be Jake again.

"Come on," he said finally, and headed toward the door.

In the corner of my eye, I could see Vanessa watching us. For the first time in a long while, I felt a flutter of hope.

We rounded the corner and Jake leaned against a lamppost, staring up at the sky. I sat down on a fire hydrant and looked up at him, unsure of what to say.

"I'm not dating Cecily anymore, in case you're wondering," he said, still not looking at me. "She broke up with me actually—I know you were concerned about her feelings."

I deserved that.

"Are you dating Vanessa?" I hadn't meant to ask, but I was too curious not to.

"Why do you care? Or are you just worried about her stealing Colin away?"

I deserved that, too.

"No, to answer your question. Vanessa's an artist. This is business. That's all."

"Colin and I aren't together anymore. He was cheating on me the whole time with Cecily." I could tell he was startled by that last bit, but he quickly recovered.

"I'm sorry to hear that."

"I was wrong about them, Jake. I've been wrong about a lot of things."

More silence.

"So why did you come tonight?" he asked finally.

"Because I wanted to see you."

"Why's that?"

"Because you're my friend." I looked down. "My best friend."

"Lena, I didn't paint that picture of you."

"You didn't?" I was confused.

"Nick painted that picture. It was from a long time ago."

"He did?" My stomach fell flat. "I just thought—"

"I know what you thought. I know exactly how you think. God, Lena, you're thinking I painted that picture and that means that I'm going to forget about what happened between us and we'll just go back to normal. We can't go back. You can't expect me to follow your imagination's story line. It doesn't work that way."

"Jake, please just let me—"

But Jake wasn't listening. He kicked the lamppost with his foot and lit up a cigarette. "God, Lena, do you think I *wanted* to confront you at Colin's house? Of course not. But you were so wrapped up in him, I could never get in touch with you. Do you know how completely freaked out *I* was?"

"Freaked out by what? What was it?"

"Oh my God." He looked at me now. "You still don't get it?"

"Get what, Jake? Tell me," I said, my eyes searching his.

"Lena, that night, I was trying to tell you." He stopped himself.

"What? Please." I moved toward him.

He looked me in the eyes. "I was going to tell you that I loved you," he said.

I felt my whole body go numb. I couldn't breathe.

"When you feel something like that, you can't wait for the *appropriate time* to express it," he said.

I looked down, too overcome to meet his gaze.

"Maybe you'll feel that way about somebody someday, Lena."

And with that, Jake turned and walked away. Again.

"Scotch and soda, please." I took a seat at the end of the bar. After my conversation with Jake, I walked aimlessly around downtown until I found myself standing in front of Super Si's bar. It seemed right—I needed to think and this place centered me better than yoga. The nighttime crowd was younger and livelier than the daytime scene, but it was still fairly empty.

"Well, well, well, drinking alone, I see." That English accent sounded familiar. Nick? God, it was becoming difficult to be anonymous in this city.

"I could say the same for you, Nick." Judging by the look of him, the last thing he needed was a drink. His eyes were bloodshot, he could use a good shave, and the fresh smear of ink from the stamp on the back of his hand made me wonder if he had rolled out of the nearest club.

"I saw you at Jake's party earlier. What made you rush off

so quickly?" he asked, and for a second I wondered if he had seen me talking to Jake.

"I guess I wasn't in the mood. Why are you here, anyway?" I asked, not caring whether I sounded rude.

"Well, as a matter of fact, I'm here to have a celebratory drink. And, ironically enough, I have you to thank." He took the seat beside me. "Barkeep, one flute of your best champagne, *s'il vous plaît.*" He tapped the bar for emphasis.

"What are you talking about?"

"You, my dear, made me a cool five grand tonight."

"Don't be funny, Nick. It doesn't work for you."

"Do I look like I'm trying to be funny?" he said, unable to stop the smirk from spreading across his face. I didn't answer.

The bartender placed Nick's champagne down on the bar. It was in a wineglass with the words "Holiday Cheers 1996" printed in chipping green and red paint.

"Well, if you must know, your adoring friend Jake just bought my portrait of you."

"What?"

"You heard me." Nick took a very festive swig of champagne and laughed. "He actually got into a rather nasty bidding war with a very nice retired couple from Westchester. They were about to close on it, but he dashed over, put his teeth in and wouldn't let go."

"He did?" I said with disbelief.

"He did, indeed. And the funny thing is, he's my dealer now. He's supposed to be making money *off* of me, not giving it to me!" Nick was lost in the memory, his face shiny with glee and greed. "Glad I finally got a return on investment for our rather dismal relationship," he said.

But I wasn't listening. All I could think about was Jake.

"He's a real knight in shining armor, that one," Nick snorted as he slung back another swallow of champagne.

"What are you talking about?"

"Oh God, Lena. Don't play dumb with me."

"What do you mean?"

"I mean, when are you two gonna stop fucking around and just get it the fuck over with? It's annoying."

"That's a lovely sentiment, thanks, Nick."

"Jesus, it was bad enough having to put up with your ridiculous charade when we were dating, but just be real for once."

"You think I want to go out with Jake?"

"For Christ's sake, yes. And he's practically obsessed with you. Back when we were together, his girl Mandy or Mindy, the one with the dog—"

"Miranda."

"Yeah, Miranda. We used to joke about it."

"Miranda was always paranoid."

"Whatever, Lena." He thought for a moment. "Hey, is she single now?"

"Look, this is crazy. I love Jake, but—"

"But what? Why do you make everything so goddamn complicated?"

"I don't. It's not complicated. We just know each other too well."

"Let me get this straight. You're saying that you know him inside out and that you love him, but the idea of taking it further is out of the question."

"Yes, that is what I'm saying."

"Lena, darling, if I may be completely frank with you, I think what you're saying is that you're scared shitless."

I wasn't sure how best to respond to that, so I just went with, "Oh God, why am I even talking about this with you?"

"You're just pissed because I have you figured out and you can't stand it," he said, the smirk returning to his face.

"You think you've got me figured out?" I laughed out loud. "So then tell me, Nick, why do you think we broke up?"

"That's easy."

"Oh really. Enlighten me." This should be entertaining, I thought.

"Because we never dated."

"Come again?"

"You dated an artist named Nick, but that's about all he had to do with me. Your Nick was some kind of mythical figure who quoted Joyce and went to the symphony." His face turned sour. "That whole charade was exhausting. I was actually quite relieved to be done with it."

"You think I tried to make you into something that you weren't?"

"Bingo, as you Americans like to say. By the way, I was actually born in Scranton. I knew that would kill you if you found out while we were dating."

"Nick, you have it all wrong." I tried to sound convincing.

"Listen, as much as I'd love to continue to belabor the state of your love life with you, I have a very hot rendezvous with one Ms. Vanessa Vilroy." He finished his drink and took out his wallet.

"Vanessa Vilroy?" I repeated the name.

"Yeah, do you know her? She was at the party earlier— and she looked fucking amazing, by the way." He seemed lost in the memory of Vanessa and her sexy dress.

"I do know her, actually. You two would make quite a couple." I smiled to myself.

"Oh man, looks like I'm out of cash at the moment," Nick said as he closed his empty wallet. "You'll spot me the drink though, right, love?"

"Just like old times, love," I said.

And with a wink and a smile, Nick—or whoever he was—disappeared.

chapter 15

I had been waiting for Tess at the corner of Gansevoort and Ninth Avenue for close to half an hour. It was the night of Parker's engagement party, which also meant that it was the night I would see Greg again for the first time in five years. Tess and I had a plan, though—never, ever let each other out of our sight. We would arrive together, mingle together and, in general, save each other from either tedious or traumatic interactions.

The very idea that I would be sharing oxygen and finger food with Greg Olin within the hour was too much for me to comprehend. I couldn't even imagine what he looked like now. When I tried, all I could come up with was a hazy picture of a balding and bloated blank-faced man, albeit one who was still wearing Tevas and Levi's, a backward baseball cap, and a Jansport backpack.

With all the recent chaos in my life, I hadn't really had the time to properly obsess over our imminent reunion. I had, however, found the time to obsess over my outfit for the evening and had purchased a wildly expensive black Versace dress, cleverly rationalizing the cost as the price one must pay to calm one's nerves. My cardinal rule—if you can't rise above, at least look like you've risen to another income bracket.

I looked at my watch. Where *was* Tess? We were officially late and I noticed the neighborhood's working "girls" were beginning to start their shifts on the corner. I tapped my foot and made accidental eye contact with a slow-moving BMW that had circled the block at least twice before. The driver stopped the car in front of me. Oh God, what do I do? (I was not a little offended that he mistook my high fashion for transvestite hooker-wear.)

"Hey there, are you looking for a date?" A pasty middle-aged man leaned out the window lecherously.

Wasn't that supposed to be my line? I thought to myself.

"Uh…" I mean, I *was* looking for a date. When wasn't I looking for a date?

"You look like you're ready for a good time," he continued.

Okay, that was far enough. I should just cut to the chase.

"I'm a woman," I said with finality. I was sure of that, at least.

He examined me for a second as though I might not be telling the truth. Jesus, this was not the self-esteem boost that I needed before reuniting with my ex-boyfriend and engaging in the painful task of premarital revelry for hours on end.

"Damn bitch," he said, slamming on the accelerator, spraying a thick mist of mud all over my outfit. Men.

"Lena?"

Tess called my name as she got out of a cab.

"Lena, who was in that car?"

"Some guy who thought I was a transvestite prostitute," I said plaintively as I looked at my dress in disbelief.

"I see," she said.

"What am I going to do about my outfit?" Let's get to the important matters first, I thought.

"Oh honey." Tess leaned over to inspect the damage. "I'm so sorry I'm late." She glanced at her watch. "There's no time to go home—it's ten till nine."

"That's okay—how bad is it?" I moaned but felt so much better already, glad that Tess was there to be the mom of the situation, to listen to me whine and to make everything right again.

"We'll go straight to the bathroom when we get there. I'll fix it and it'll be good as new," she said.

My heart rested. Tess would take care of it. And then…

"Hey there. I'm sorry we're late." A beautiful man emerged like a phoenix from Tess's cab. His bronzed, muscular arms encircled Tess. Macho Macchiato.

"Lena, this is Marcel," Tess said.

I stared back at him, transfixed (partly by surprise and partly by his utter gorgeousness). Tess eyed me nervously.

"Hi there. It's great to meet you." I extended my scrawny, chalk-white hand, which he enthusiastically shook with his warm, beautiful one.

"It's really a pleasure to meet you, too." He even sounded like he meant it.

He was wearing a tie. He was coming with us. I was glad for Tess—this was big for her. She'd come to an emotional crossroads and had made it to the other side. She had found someone who she actually had a passion for, was invested in, someone meaningful to her who was able to seep beneath her cynical surface.

But for God's sake, did it have to be tonight? I needed cover!
I couldn't saunter around the room with a couple. That would
perhaps be the only scenario worse than showing up alone.

"Are we ready?" Tess looked at me, thanking me with
her eyes.

"Yes," I said, my game face in full effect.

And off we went, the three of us, to the party.

The restaurant, Panacea (Danny Meyer's latest), was packed
so I could hardly see beyond the cluster of blown-out blondes
in front of me. I felt the familiar anxiety that I always experienced when I walked into a social event of this level. I was
at one of my best friend's engagement party—a party that I
had practically co-produced—and I still felt slightly intimidated. I needed to be confident. I needed to be in control. I
needed a bathroom stall, and a stain stick, for the love of God.

As soon as we walked through the door, Tess had been
enveloped by at least ten people who "just *had* to say hello,"
which really meant that they just *had* to quiz her about her
newly acquired arm candy. Even in this room, Macho Macchiato stood out.

I navigated my way through the throng of people, searching for my beacon of hope, a bathroom, brushing off the
inevitable stares at my chest (a new thing for me, certainly),
some of the more trend-obsessed wondering if mud
splashes were the new thing, no doubt.

And that's when I saw him. He sat at the bar, cupping a beer.
The past five years could have been rendered nonexistent at
that moment. I could have just come from a long research session at the library. He could have just gotten out of class. We
could be meeting up for another lazy night of drinking too
much and talking about everything and nothing at the same
time. Time just seemed to move more slowly back then.

He wasn't bald and he wasn't bloated. He was handsome, still—perhaps more so. And he was well dressed. Of course he was. And I was standing six feet away, caked in mud, with the bathroom accessible only by crossing directly through his line of vision. The evening was off to a splendid start!

I inhaled deeply, straightened my shoulders and assumed the rigid posture of one who is about to dive into a pool of freezing water.

"Greg?" I said, dizzy with the surrealness of his proximity.

"Lena?" He smiled. "I can't believe it's you."

I felt a warm rush of familiarity and the instant dissolution of anything bitter or unseemly that may have transpired between us. Why had I dreaded seeing him? It was all a mystery to me now.

"Do you want to grab a table?" he asked, still beaming.

"Sure." And I meant it.

We headed over to one of the few free tables left, which bore a red sign marked "Reserved"—only Parker would set aside a VIP area at her own engagement party. I plucked the sign away and placed it on a passing waiter's tray.

"Breaking the rules?" Greg teased.

"I know the host," I responded.

"You always were a rebel," he said. "You ran off to New York, after all."

Just like that, we slipped effortlessly back into our comfortable repartee. It felt so comforting to use phrases like "Remember that time" and "That's so like you."

The din around us dulled to a whisper as I listened intently. He filled me in on the missing five years, this strange separation that now required us to quickly fill in the blanks so that we could again say we knew absolutely everything about each other.

He had hung around school for a while after graduation, not sure what to do. Eventually he moved up to Jackson Hole with some other similarly wayward post grads with an ambition for little but to further hone their hobbies. He had gotten to know one of his ski students, a banker, who took a liking to him, offered him a job, which he took, and which he discovered he did well. Long story short, he had moved to corporate headquarters in Chicago, and was quickly working his way up the ladder there.

My turn went as well as it could, I thought. He laughed at my small-town girl in the big city stories, my Nadine stories, my Parker and Tess stories. I glossed over my broken heart/world turned upside down predicament and he admirably did not probe for details.

"It's just so weird to see you again," I marveled, resting my chin on my hand as I, once again, took it all in. I felt relaxed for the first time in a long time. "Where do you think we went wrong?" I asked before I could ponder whether it was appropriate.

"Oh, Lena, that was all so long ago."

"No, I'm serious. What happened to us?"

"We were young. Neither of us really knew what we wanted, I don't think."

"Did I try to make you into something that you weren't?" I asked.

"No, of course not," he said, but I could tell by the way he bit his lip that he was lying.

"Greg, just tell me. I kind of need to know."

"Lena, this is silly," he said.

"It's not silly. I wanted to move to New York and I couldn't understand why you didn't. I couldn't imagine why you would want any other life than the one I wanted," I said.

"Yeah," he said, finally. "But we both know I was a little lost back then. I could have used some direction," he said.

"Oh Greg, that's so not true. I was just living in a dream world. I guess I couldn't see what was right in front of me," I said.

"Lena, I have to tell you something," Greg said nervously.

"What do you think would happen if we just sat down here tonight and started over," I wondered out loud.

"Started over?" Greg sounded confused.

"Yeah, like we put our old relationship aside and started fresh? A whole new thing. Can people do that?"

"Well, I don't—"

"If they're fully invested and honest with each other?"

"Lena, please just let me—"

"Don't you think? I mean, is that possible? Can two people redefine a relationship after knowing each other for so long?" My mind was churning now.

Greg rested his head in his hands.

"I mean, the fact of the matter is we already know all the bad stuff about each other. We'd just build on the good—"

"Lena," Greg interrupted suddenly. "I'm actually seeing someone. Her name's Beth. We just started dating, but I have a really good feeling about it and as great as it is to see you again—"

"Oh, Greg! That's wonderful!"

"It is?" He looked confused.

"Wait." I thought for a moment. "Did you think I was coming on to you?"

"You weren't?"

"No!" I said. "Oh, no. No, no, no!" I wanted to laugh. "You thought I meant us? No! I was thinking about just the *idea*," I said. In reality of course, I was thinking about Jake.

If I could imagine being friends with Greg after having a relationship for so many years, why couldn't I have a relationship with Jake after being friends for so long?

"Oh, thank God," Greg said, palpably relieved.

We shared a look and then both started laughing.

"You really had me worried there," he said.

"You poor thing!" I said sympathetically.

"You know what, Lena Sharpe." Greg looked at me now. "You haven't changed a bit."

And that's where Greg was wrong. I had changed so much—I was only recently beginning to realize just how much. The old me would have looked at Greg, sitting in front of me bathed in nostalgia and flattering candlelight, and would have wondered: Is he the one? Is this a sign? Are we meant to be? But I didn't have to wonder and I didn't have to conjure images of our hypothetical life together. I was a completely different person than the girl Greg was remembering so tenderly right now. I liked her, too, I remembered her fondly, but I was finally ready to let her go.

"Excuse me, I believe this is our table."

I turned my head in a way that, in hindsight, I feel must have had the dramatic effect of the cinematic slow motion used to depict, say, Lindsay Wagner morphing into the Bionic Woman or perhaps that seminal *Brady Bunch* episode in which Marcia gets hit in the nose by a football.

It was Sienna Skye.

Oh no, it doesn't end there. It gets better….

Slinking behind her, looking like a pathetic column of corduroy and cowardice, was…Colin Bates.

"Oh my God! What is on your breasts?" Sienna squealed.

I looked over at Greg, but his gaze was locked steadily on the other pair of breasts involved in this conversation.

"It's mud," I answered, feeling my voice grow stronger as

I elaborated without prompting. "I was mistaken for a male prostitute on the street earlier and his car sprayed mud on me when he sped off after realizing that I was a woman."

Greg's mouth hung agape. Colin's face was ashen.

"So, like, we need this table right now." Sienna was back on track. And then, by way of explanation of her authority I suppose, she added, "The groom happens to be one of my lawyers."

I was wondering why she was here.

"I don't think so," I replied, ostensibly to Sienna, but my eyes remained fixated on Colin. I was not afraid. But I could tell he was. He started to slink away.

"Oh, Colin," I called out to him.

He froze in his footsteps.

"May I speak with you for a moment?"

I didn't wait for an answer as I grabbed his arm and led him to a corner. I really didn't know what I was going to say to him. I just knew I had to say something.

"Lena, I should explain." Colin shifted his feet, trying his luck at a preemptive strike.

"Okay," I said.

He paused, clearly not expecting the opportunity and clearly unprepared for it. "I just want you to know that the feelings that I had for you—the feelings that I think we shared for each other—" he looked at me for affirmation "—were completely, entirely real. Absolutely. It's just that Cecily, well…" He lowered his voice as if he were about to share some information in confidence with me. "She's going through a rough patch right now and I just couldn't. Well, you know. You're a sensitive person, after all." He ran his fingers through his hair. "And so, this thing with Sienna is just, you know, it's just really nothing, is what it is. She just, you know, likes my writing and wanted to talk to me about it.

It's really just a professional meeting, in a sense. A real sense. I know you're hurting but you're going to feel much less awful about everything as soon as time has passed and you have, you know, healed. So, I just want to say that, well, I forgive you. I want to do that for you."

I realized in that moment that if I had been guilty of visiting my imagination a little too often, then Colin had apparently taken up full-time residence in his.

"*You* forgive *me?*"

He nodded his head and smiled beneficently. "Absolutely."

"City Boy." I spat the words at him. They expressed my contempt perfectly. There was nothing else I wanted to say to him, so I turned and walked away.

"Wait? That was you?" I could hear him try to follow me, but he must have gotten tangled in the crowd, because his voice just faded away into nothing.

"Lena! I am so proud of you! Lena Sharpe!" I felt a tug at my dress and I turned to see none other than an out-of-breath Sheila Sunshine smiling wildly at me. She was wrapped in blue chiffon and her hair was pulled up in what appeared to be a "special occasion" silver scrunchy. Despite her formal wear, she still carried a canvas tote, crowded with buttons encouraging early mammograms and reproductive freedoms.

"Sheila? I didn't expect to see you here," I said. Wow, this party was just full of surprise special guests.

"Lena!" She sounded winded. "Was that Colin you were just with in the corner?"

"Yes, as a matter of fact, it was," I said, wondering how she figured that out.

"I knew it! I have an instinct about these things," she said, beaming. "Your body language was amazing, I have to say. You've learned so much!"

As much as I wanted to roll my eyes at Sheila and tell her that I didn't buy into any of her "life coaching" techniques, I couldn't. She looked so small and vulnerable standing in front of me, her eyes filled with genuine goodwill. Sheila Sunshine was on my side. Maybe that's why Parker got such comfort from her. Maybe that's all a person really needs at the end of the day.

"Thanks, Sheila. You helped me a lot," I said.

"You helped yourself, Lena." She smiled up at me. "Now, what's next for you?"

"I don't know exactly. But it's all about the future, not the past. You certainly got that right."

"You're going to be just fine. I can sense that about you," Sheila said with a wink. "Now, go have some fun tonight."

"That sounds like a great idea. If you'll excuse me, I have to go congratulate the bride-to-be," I said, noticing Parker out of the corner of my eye. I moved toward her, but the closer I got, the more I could sense that something wasn't right.

"Parker, what's wrong?" I said when I finally reached her.

"Everything." She grabbed my wrist and I noticed her eyes were damp. Tears? This was in public, this was her moment, and she didn't say anything about the mud on my dress. This was not Parker.

Parker pulled me through the crowds of people, almost all of whom attempted to win her attention, offer their congratulations and gasp at her engagement ring. She expertly weaved through the crowd, never stopping for a beat as she air-kissed, beamed and waved her way through the assemblage of revelers. Finally we reached the kitchen and, as the swinging doors swished behind us, it was if they had flicked a switch. Parker began to cry.

"Parker, what is it? What happened?" I had never seen

her cry before. Had anyone? She hunched over, clutching her stomach. It occurred to me that she might have appendicitis. I steered her away from the trail of bow-tied waiters, marching in formation in and out of the kitchen.

"Carlos, we need more pâté, not so much crudités," Parker instructed the head waiter with her last breath before collapsing on a sack of flour and launching into a suspended stretch of heaving and moaning.

"Parker, are you okay? Are you sick?"

She shook her head, which was now buried in her hands. We sat like that for a few minutes. In time, she raised her head again and looked at me. Her brows furrowed together (as much as they could given her prenuptial Botox treatments), her lips parted slowly, her eyes searched mine…and then she was gripped by another fit of tears.

"There you are, Lena. I'm so sorry we got separated!" Tess burst through the doors, looking exuberant, but she immediately sobered at the sight of Parker.

"Parker, what happened?"

Parker didn't answer and I could only offer a confused shrug and a concerned look. Tess pulled up an empty wine crate beside us and took a seat. And there we sat. Finally, deliberately, Parker spoke.

"I can't get married," she said. An eerie calmness had crept into her voice.

"Why not?" Tess asked, in such a way that implied we were ready and able to smooth away any anxiety or allay any fear.

Parker didn't hesitate and her voice didn't waiver. "You know how they always say, 'When you know you've found the one, you just know.' Well, I know. And Brad is not the one."

"Parker, it is completely normal to be nervous before something as major as marriage," I said, but now she was making *me* nervous.

"But I don't love him," she said. "And I don't think he loves me, either."

The words hung in the air between us.

Her tone made things clear. This wasn't last-minute fears or prenuptial jitters. This wasn't Parker drama. Brad hadn't worn the wrong shoes or picked the wrong restaurant. He was the wrong man. It was as simple—and as complicated—as that.

Parker had spent the past year and a half picking just the right shade of ivory invitations (not too eggshell-ish, but certainly not ecru), just the right butter-cream to ice the cake (not too sour, but not too sweet), just the right bows for the flower girls' hair (not too garish, but not too plain). She had gotten only one thing wrong. The groom.

"Have you talked to him?" I asked gently.

"We just talked."

"And what did he say?"

She paused. "It's more what he didn't say." She looked forlorn. "He wasn't devastated. He wasn't traumatized. He just stood there, sort of like he was annoyed."

"He's probably in shock. It's just his way of dealing with things," Tess countered.

"No." Parker was firm. "It's just *him*."

I was certainly in shock. Parker and Brad always seemed to be a fait accompli. He had all the preliminary qualifications that she required: Ivy League undergrad (double major in econ and poly sci), top twenty law school (a little bit of trouble with that NY bar exam, but everyone knows it's the toughest and the third time was the charm, so…), good-looking but not ostentatiously so, good family, good teeth, fiscally conservative but socially liberal, adept at home repair. Perfect. Sure, they argued, but Parker argued with everyone. And Brad was a lawyer, which meant he argued for a living.

More importantly, it was Parker's *time*. Her life had un-
folded in the orderly progression of a prix fixe dinner. Boarding school—Prom Queen—College—Serious boyfriend—
Cohabitation—and then finally, inevitably (cue chorus) Marriage. If Parker didn't get married, my whole view of the
universe would be altered. She was that girl in the Sunday
Times wedding section with the perfect pedigree, the perfect résumé, and the perfect groom. I was the one who was
supposed to be searching, wondering, hoping for that missing piece of the puzzle, that ideal, hypothetical someone
who, I was half convinced, would fall directly from the sky
onto the park bench in front of me (when I was wearing lip
gloss and enjoying a clear complexion).

We sat there splayed out like starfish, silently contem-
plating what had brought us to this moment.

"Parker, where is all this coming from?" Tess said, delicately.

"I was daydreaming," she responded after a moment.

"What do you mean exactly?" I asked.

Parker leaned her head back and looked up at the ceiling. "We were sitting at brunch today. We weren't talking
about the wedding or his job stress and we weren't arguing
about any of the things we usually argue about. We were
just sitting there." Her voice got quieter. "I started watching the other people around us—the families and the couples and I realized that we were the only ones not talking.
And then I got this image in my head of the two of us sitting across from each other, thirty years from now, silent. The
sad truth is that Brad and I really don't have a lot to say to
each other." She raised her head to look at us. "Does that
make sense?"

"Yeah, it does," I said quietly as Tess nodded.

"It wasn't supposed to be this way," Parker said.

But any of us could have said it. We had all been mov-

ing in fits and starts toward what we believed to be our pre-
scribed fates, our "destinies." And then something—everything—had changed. It was like watching a movie and the
picture suddenly goes to black—but when it comes back on,
a completely different film appears.

"God, what am I going to do?" Parker said quietly.

"Honey, you're going to be fine. I'm just so proud of you
for facing this head-on," Tess said.

"She's right, Parker. Do you know how many people
wouldn't be brave enough to do what you just did?"

"I don't feel brave. I feel stupid. Every single person in
this restaurant is going to think I'm a flake."

"Parker." I sat up on my flour sack and leaned toward her.
"All this wedding stuff…pretty much *everything* on the other
side of these swinging doors, is just a fantasy. You're dealing with what's real. And most people never want to face
that. I certainly didn't."

"But now you have?" Parker said softly.

"Now I'm starting to," I said.

"Me, too," Tess added.

"God, look at the three of us." Parker smiled. "There's a
great party out there and we're all hiding in the kitchen."
Then she gathered herself together, making clear that her
time to wallow had come to an end. "Okay, I've got to go
out there for the toast."

"Oh honey, don't you think you can probably skip the
toast?" Tess said.

"No." She was resolute. "This is an engagement party so
there must be an engagement toast."

Tess and I shared a nervous look.

"Plus, I'm dying to try this vintage champagne that I
managed to buy wholesale from Veuve Cliquot." Parker's
eyes lit up, remembering her score.

Parker was going to be all right. She'd have some explaining to do, but she'd be all right.

We all got up, dusted ourselves off, and marched out the kitchen's swinging doors like Charlie's Angels. I made a beeline for the bathroom—finally. Once inside, I grabbed a stack of paper towels, secured myself in a stall and got to work. It felt so good to be alone.

As if on cue, I heard the bathroom door swing open and the staccato clip of heels on linoleum. A cell phone rang and I soon realized that I was listening, once again, to the shrill sounds of Sienna Skye.

"Hi, Whitney, thanks for calling me back. I'm *dying* here."

Okay, this could be interesting. I peered through the crack in the stall's door to see Sienna bent over the sink examining her pores in the mirror. Did Sienna Skye have pores? Maybe she was trying to figure that out herself.

"I mean, Jesus Christ, if I hear one more word about that stupid book, you know? I'm like, try making three movies in one year *and* balance a recurring role on the WB's hottest teen drama."

There was a pause and then a loud cackle as Sienna vociferously agreed with Whitney's response.

"And you know—he's so not as cute as Nadine said."

Nadine set this up? Of course.

"And he's totally losing his hair."

Right on, sister! I felt a sudden urge for a high five.

"You're so right." Sienna was nodding her head. Apparently, Whitney was rife with wisdom. "I knooooow!" Sienna was off on another laughing fit, during which she dropped her lip gloss, which rolled off the counter and over toward the stall next to me. I repositioned myself, careful not to be caught. As I was leaning against the door, I caught sight of Sienna Skye bending down to retrieve the wayward gloss, her micromini edging up her Hawaiian Tropic legs.

What I saw next would change my view of the world from that moment forward, it would sustain my belief in justice and equality for all of womankind, it would reinvigorate my hope for myself and my future. Sienna Skye had cellulite.

I emerged from the bathroom with a smile on my face, a mud-free dress (well, less muddy, anyway) and a spring in my step. Spotting fat deposits on a stick-thin starlet can really lift one's spirits, I decided. I made my way to the bar and took a seat, surveying the crowd. Off to my left, I saw a lone couple dancing intimately.

"I give them two months." I recognized the voice behind me. "If the weather stays nice, maybe three."

"Why do you say that?" I said, without turning. "I think they look very happy together."

"I've always admired your optimism." He paused. "I know I did my very best to make you cynical."

"I didn't expect you to be here tonight," I said, turning around to look at him for the first time.

"I didn't think I would, either," he said.

"So, why did you come?" I asked.

"Well, I knew my best friend would be here." He paused for a moment, "and I needed to apologize to her." He looked down at me. "Lena, I'm so sorry."

"Not as sorry as I am," I said, tears streaming down my face. "Jake, did you really buy Nick's portrait of me?"

"I did," he said. "And you're one lucky girl, I might add. If I hadn't swooped down and bought it, your face would have ended up above a sectional sofa in Scarsdale. Probably in a rec room," he said with a shiver.

I laughed. It felt so good to laugh with Jake again.

Jake leaned forward and wiped my face gently with a napkin. "You're going to scare that guy away if you don't clean yourself up here," he teased me.

"What guy?"

"That guy, standing by the coat check who hasn't taken his eyes off you since you walked up to the bar."

Instinctively I turned to look. The guy in question, a Jude Law look-alike, immediately turned away, embarrassed.

"What makes you think I'd like him?"

"Because I know you, Lena."

"You do know me. Better than I know myself sometimes, right?" I held his gaze for one brief moment.

"Okay, would you stop making me beg here for you to go talk to the hot guy in the corner?" he said, breaking the tension. "I already feel like Duckie in *Pretty in Pink*."

"I don't want to talk to that guy," I said.

"You don't?"

"No," I said firmly.

"Why not?"

"Because he's a firefly."

"He's a what?"

"Nothing. Because I'd rather stay here and talk to you."

We stood like that for a moment, watching the couple dance in front of us.

"So, tell me. Why do you think this couple won't last?" I asked.

He paused. "Because I know them. And I know they were friends first and that they just sort of fell into a relationship."

"That's not a reason."

He turned to look at me. "It's not?" he said. He seemed so vulnerable, so un-Jake-like.

"No."

"But what if it doesn't work?"

"But what if it does?"

"It could change things."

"It could change everything."

We were staring at each other now, the dancing couple long forgotten.

"Did I ever tell you—" Jake moved in closer, his confidence was back "—how amazing you are?"

"I think you did," I said, looking up at him. "But I was too preoccupied to listen."

"And now?"

"Now I'm ready."

"Well, how do we do this?"

"We don't do anything," I said. "Don't anticipate. Just follow the music."

And with that, we joined the dancing couple, out on the floor. Taking our turn. Just another two singles, trying their luck as a pair.

5,4,3,2,1… Rolling

Cue Music—

Kelly Karaway, Host: Hello and welcome everyone to *Face to Face*. I'm Kelly Karaway. I'd like to take this opportunity to introduce you to our newest *Face to Face* correspondent—Lena Sharpe. Each week, she'll be bringing you a slice of "real life" as she hosts "Reality Check," a new segment for the show. Hello and welcome, Lena!

Lena Sharpe, Correspondent: Thanks, Kelly.

Kelly Karaway: Tell us all about this exciting new segment, Lena.

Lena Sharpe: Well, Kelly, the idea is to shine the spotlight on some interesting people that you likely haven't heard of before.

Kelly Karaway: Everyday people?

Lena Sharpe: That's one way of putting it.

Kelly Karaway: Mmm…that's so *real*. Why don't you give us a sneak peek at what's coming up.

Lena Sharpe: Sure. Our first segment profiles Svetlana Ostrakov. She's currently a waitress at an East Village restaurant, but, in her former life, she was a principle dancer in the Kirov Ballet. We're going to take a look at her life and hear some of her wisdom.

Kelly Karaway: That's fascinating, Lena. So you mean to tell me that I could just go downtown and order a cup of coffee from her right now?

Lena Sharpe: That's right.

Kelly Karaway: Well, I might just do that! I can't wait to hear her stories.

Lena Sharpe: Yes, well, everyone has a story, Kelly. That's what "Reality Check" is all about.

Kelly Karaway: Now tell me, Lena Sharpe, what's your story?

Lena Sharpe: That's an interesting question, Kelly. I think my story is still unfolding, and I can honestly say that I can't wait to find out what happens next.

CUT